VENGEANCE ON HIGH

A Wally Morris Mystery

•

Joani Ascher

AVALON BOOKS
NEW YORK

Published by Thomas Bouregy & Co., Inc.
160 Madison Avenue, New York, NY 10016

Library of Congress Cataloging-in-Publication Data

Ascher, Joani.
Vengeance on high : a Wally Morris mystery / Joani Ascher.
p. cm.
ISBN 0-8034-9769-5 (alk. paper)
1. Morris, Wally (Fictitious character)—Fiction. I. Title.

PS3601.S29V466 2006
813'.6—dc22
2005035219

PRINTED IN THE UNITED STATES OF AMERICA
ON ACID-FREE PAPER
BY HADDON CRAFTSMEN, BLOOMSBURG, PENNSYLVANIA

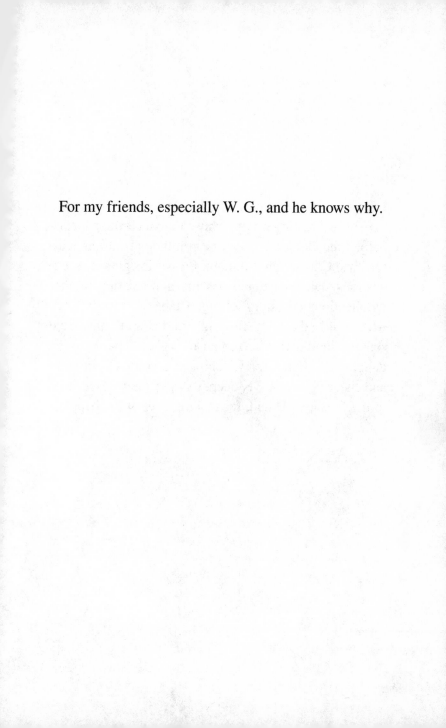

For my friends, especially W. G., and he knows why.

I am grateful to Deborah Nolan and Kim Zito, members of my writing group, whose guidance and patience helped me along the way. My gratitude also to my editor, Erin Cartwright-Niumata, for her insights and suggestions. Janet Toledano has my appreciation for her recollections and story telling. Thanks to my son, Ari, who could take a woefully misguided and convoluted sentence and turn it into concise English. Thanks to my daughter, Shonna, for watching my story's continuity and cheering me on. My deepest appreciation, as always, to my husband, David, for making everything happen.

Chapter One

"Do you see them?" Wally Morris asked as she hurried beside her husband, Nate. They were walking among hundreds of people, all headed in the same direction and it was almost impossible to see.

Nate looked around. "Down there. Louise is waving." He took Wally by the arm and steered her along.

When Wally and Nate arrived, summer dusk was just settling over a park filled with people awaiting Grosvenor's yearly July Fourth spectacular. The warm, slightly moist atmosphere hung close, although the humidity was lower than it had been earlier in the afternoon. The air hummed with the sounds of bees and mosquitoes heading for a human feast, and people, thousands of them, speaking in scores of different languages. Many of the people wore clothing that matched their ethnicities, such as saris, dashikis, turbans, hijabs, and African head wraps. Everyone bubbled with anticipation.

The Morrises picked their way through a sea of blankets, folding lounge chairs, and running children until they found their place among several of their friends.

"I hope you're handling the heat better than we are," said Cameron Buxton, shaking Nate's hand. With his other hand he wiped his forehead.

"Your contractor still hasn't finished putting in the central air conditioning?" Wally asked Cameron's wife, Cyd.

Cyd shook her head. "It was bad planning to start it in April. The contractor kept running into concrete walls that no one knew were there. It's been a nightmare."

Wally commiserated for a moment, then she and Nate moved on to Marty and Leigh Fried. "How did you do at the show?" Nate asked Marty.

"Okay, I guess."

"I'd say it was more than okay," Wally said. She had really enjoyed Marty's first one-man show. "The photos were wonderful."

"He's being too modest," Leigh said. "The show was great. Many of the photographs sold, although it turns out someone," she nodded in Marty's direction, "wasn't ready to part with them."

"Can't you just print more?" Wally asked, hoping her ignorance wasn't showing.

"Of course he can," said Leigh. "But I bet he won't. He'll have moved into a whole new phase—the Africa phase. I'm sure he'll have plenty to work with after our trip."

"When do you leave?" Wally asked.

Marty beamed. "The limousine will be at the house at six tomorrow morning. We fly to London first, and then on to Africa."

"Have a great time, you two," said Wally. "I have to admit, I'm jealous." She worked her way down to the clear spot at the edge of the group of couples to sit next to her closest friend, Louise Fisch.

The group had been attending this event at Berten Park together for as long as most of them had lived in Grosvenor, New Jersey. But unlike in years past, when everyone was mellow from a long barbeque at the home of one of the group, full of children and noise, each couple had gone its own way for the day. As dutiful and loving grandparents, Wally and Nate had spent theirs with their daughter, Rachel, and son-in-law, Adam, and their granddaughter, Jody, at their house in Westchester, an hour away. Rachel was due to deliver her second child in four weeks and Wally's excitement was mounting daily.

Louise put her long red hair into a clip and stuffed it under a baseball cap. "That will keep the mosquitoes off my head," she said, adding a spritz of bug repellant. "I can't stand the little buggers."

"Give me a shot," Nate said, tilting his silvery head toward her. "I think Wally missed the top."

"I don't see how I could have not missed," said Wally, "since you wouldn't bend down." As vertically challenged as Wally was, especially in relation to her over six-foot-tall husband, she didn't bother feeling guilty. She spread her blanket to sit facing the valley where the fireworks would be launched and pulled Nate down next to her.

Louise turned to her husband, Norman, with her insect repellent poised to squirt him. He shook his head, and tipped his Yankees cap. "I'm good, thanks anyway." Louise finished her preparations and put everything away in a large tote bag. Norman sighed with apparent relief and fell into conversation with Nate.

"How are the newlyweds?" Louise asked Wally.

Wally's and Nate's second daughter, Debbie, had married Elliot Levine in June of the previous year. "I wouldn't call them newlyweds anymore," Wally reminded Louise. "They just couldn't fit in the actual honeymoon until now, since they wanted to go away for so long. And in answer to your question, we haven't heard a thing."

Louise swept a stray red hair off her neck, fanned herself and smiled. "They must be having a fabulous time."

Nate settled in beside Wally and looked over at Norman. "How are things coming along with the museum bid?"

"Good," Norman said. "We've got all our ducks in a row and everything has been filed. Gabe Ferry did a good job on the exhibit proposal, and the town engineers have certified that the designated house has no violations. The deadline is July 31st, and then I guess we'll know."

Norman was chairing a committee that had applied for a grant being offered to one of four towns along the Morris-Essex rail line. Each town had an old mansion that was a candidate for restoration to its original mid-nineteenth century condition. Only one would get the go ahead, which came with more than a houseful of period furnishings and artifacts.

"What are our chances?"

"I think they're okay. We've probably got a better chance than Chatham. Summit may have an edge because of the hotel, and maybe Madison, too, but a little birdie told me—"

"That would be me," Louise chimed in.

"Right," said her husband, "that little birdie told me that she has a client who is looking at another nearby mansion, a real fixer upper, to be kind, to convert into a bed and breakfast. That should satisfy Mrs. Hampton."

Dolores Hampton was the heir to a publishing fortune and well known in philanthropic circles for her generosity and eccentricity. Her desire to completely refurbish her own mansion was the impetus for the museum dedicated to remembering the heydays of the New York moguls who came to settle along the railroad line. That way she could donate all her old things and not feel guilty when she went shopping for new furniture, or so Wally had heard.

It came as no surprise to anyone that Dolores Hampton made it into the competition and had everyone dancing to her tune.

"I hope so," said Nate. "She's progressive and modern in wanting to redecorate her house and kind in offering to donate all her old things to a museum. She is also more than generous in helping to fix up the mansion where her collection will be housed, but from what

I heard, she is prim and proper when it comes to decorum. Any hint of scandal will sink a town's chances."

"What's happening over there?" Wally asked, looking at a particularly dense crowd on the far end of the park. It was much steeper in that section and used in the winter as a sledding hill until every speck of snow was worn off the slope.

Louise jumped out of her chair and strained closer for a look. "I think there's a brawl." Police hurrying over to the point of the altercation confirmed what Louise had said. Wally could see that it was among the opposing groups carrying placards for and against building in the abandoned quarry up near the top of the mountain on which the town of Grosvenor was built. No one had paid any attention at all to the quarry, not for years after it was shut down. Now it was a hot-button issue, ever since a local entrepreneur-turned-housing developer, Keith Hollis, purchased the land and made plans to clear it and fill it with condominiums and mini-mansions. Suddenly everyone, or at least so it seemed, had an opinion.

People opposed the building because they felt the influx of residents who would fill those housing units would overwhelm the schools and cause overcrowding. Others were against it because of traffic congestion. Gabriel Ferry, a college professor who lived high up on the hill overlooking the quarry, which was the premium real estate in town, had come out publicly on behalf of himself and his neighbors, worrying about their scenic views and quality of life. And all the groups gave loud voice to their opinions.

As the police led away whoever had been involved in the fist fight, the picketers regrouped. For a moment it looked as if another fight might erupt but the protesters soon dispersed. Norman breathed a sigh of relief. "That's just the kind of thing that could blow us out of the water for the museum."

Louise took him by the arm and told him not to worry.

Hundreds of people were still streaming into the park, carrying coolers, blankets, chairs, and babies. Little by little, as the sky darkened, teenaged vendors sold pliable light sticks, which children flocked to buy and turn into colorful, glowing necklaces, bracelets and head rings. In the growing dark, all one could see were floating halos.

Sitting and watching all the people of the town walk by was always a pleasant time for Wally. On an evening like this, with the whole town coming together to celebrate the nation's birth, the richness of the diverse community was in full view. In general, everyone got along, with the late exception of the quarry warriors. None of them got along because they all had different reasons for and against the building.

Nate, for example, had stated emphatically and at length on many occasions that clearing out the abandoned quarry and filling it with hundreds of condominiums would not only destroy the ecology of the quarry, it would disturb the wetlands that had formed and which had become a beautiful place to watch wildlife. He believed it would make a lovely park and be a good addition to the county park that abutted the community. There were many people working with him to preserve the open space. Unfortunately, Hollis, the developer, was fighting just as hard to get his own way.

At a little after nine-fifteen, people started gazing around because fireworks could be heard but not seen. Looking over Wally's shoulder in the opposite direction from the valley at the bottom of the park, Louise pointed. "Up there."

"The country club," Wally said, referring to the tennis club one block up from Berten Park. Due to the steepness of the mountain, every block from east to west was significantly higher than the one before it. It was easy to see the rooftops of the houses midway down the street from the upper corner, at least until the street curved out of sight, as did most of the streets. "They are always a few minutes ahead of the town and—"

She broke off when she spotted Keith Hollis. He was a good looking man, wearing khaki pants, a striped polo shirt and Docksiders and he strode purposely along the sidewalk at the top of the park, his appearance and pace most unlike the more casually dressed, slowly sauntering crowd.

Hoping to keep Nate's attention diverted until Hollis was out of range, Wally squirmed around to make it more convincing that she was looking at the fireworks from the country club. "Oh, look at how pretty that one is."

"You don't have to twist yourself into a pretzel," Nate chided her. "I already saw Keith. I'm not going to confront him, if that's what you think."

"I don't. You aren't the militant type. I just didn't

want to remind you of the problems. We're here to have fun."

"Yes, you two," Louise chimed in. "And I think the fireworks are about to start."

Suddenly the night sky was filled with color, slowly at first and then with increasing intensity. For the next twenty or so minutes, beautiful and varied fireworks kept the huge crowd on the hill happy. As the finale approached, more and more rockets were launched in quick succession. Then there was a lull, during which some people gathered their things to leave, turning away from the valley and the source of the fireworks, but savvy residents knew what was coming. A single blast was followed by an enormous red burst of color which turned a brilliant white, before changing to a gorgeous shade of blue. Slowly the blue dots fell, fading out as they descended. The sky returned to inky black, with the exception of the lights from airplanes going to and from nearby Newark Liberty Airport.

"Do you want to come up to our house for some ice cream?" Wally asked Louise and Norman as the mass exodus started.

Norman looked as if he was about to accept the invitation but his wife shook her head. "I have an early client tomorrow," Louise said. "And don't you have to get up early for school?"

"We call it camp in the summer," Wally told her, referring to the nursery school where she worked. "But no, I don't. We have a four-day weekend."

They had arrived at Louise's sports car which she

had parked under one of Grosvenor's signature gas lights. "Then catch some extra winks on my behalf. I'll see you soon. Good night you two," Louise added, giving Nate and Wally each a peck on the cheek. "Eat some ice cream for me."

The music for a news bulletin suddenly came onto Wally's television at eleven-fifteen, A.M., breaking into a talk show mid-sentence. Wally had no time to wonder how that sentence finished because the next words of the newscaster made the talk show subject disappear completely from her mind.

"We interrupt this program," said the man with the perfect teeth, hair, and suit, whom Wally did not recognize. He was probably a substitute due to the holiday weekend. His next words confirmed he was new to the area. "We are here this morning to tell you that in Grosvenor," which he pronounced the English way, "Grove-ner," instead of as "Gross Venner," as the locals called the town, "New Jersey, police are investigating the suspicious death of a man. We have B. J. Waters on the scene." The picture switched to an outdoor scene, and B. J. Waters could be seen standing in front of a police crime scene tape which appeared to be roping off a lot of weeds. Rescue vehicles filled the background, as well as police cars and news vans. The words *Live in Grosvenor* filled the upper left corner of the television screen.

"Police this morning are reporting that the body of a man was found at the base of a local quarry," B. J. said. "A group of budding television journalists from a summer high school program, who were documenting what would be lost if a housing development was built here, made the grisly discovery at about ten this morning." The word *Earlier* replaced *Live* and a covered body was seen being taken out of the quarry bottom and brought to a van. While the tape ran, B. J.'s voice could be heard.

"This quarry is a center of contention in the town and while police haven't confirmed it, foul play may have been involved in this death. Names aren't being released at this time, pending notification of the next of kin, but an eyewitness said the body was that of Keith Hollis, the would-be developer of the quarry. Back to you in the studio."

"Thanks, B. J." The news anchor looked into the camera. "We'll be following this story closely and we'll have more at noon, five, six, and eleven o'clock."

Wally had chills. It was unbelievable. She picked up the phone to call Nate.

Chapter Two

"Here we go again," said Captain Jaeger to Detectives Dominique Scott and Ryan Devlin. "What's going on around here?"

It was a pointless question and Dominique didn't answer it. She shot a quick warning to her partner not to answer it either. He leaned back in his chair, apparently understanding her signal.

That hadn't been the case at all on the last big investigation the two of them had conducted. Ryan was as green a detective as they came when he started working in the Grosvenor Police Department, and he had no clue how to deal with a boss like Captain Jaeger. The man was demanding and insulting, all the while expecting results.

Ryan had been hired to replace Elliot Levine, Dominique's former partner who, upon finishing law school and passing the bar, had gone to work for the

12

county prosecutor's office. In comparison, Dominique knew that Ryan did not stack up. In fact, he had made several errors in judgment. Jaeger had given him every reason to believe he'd be out of there in a heartbeat if he messed up again.

Jaeger didn't wait for an answer from the two detectives in front of him. "This is a political time bomb," he said. "People are going to ask, 'Is this the way they take care of controversy in Grosvenor?' They're going to think those stories are true about the corruption that seems to be normal in every nook and cranny of New Jersey." He slapped the top of his desk. "Our reputation as a state is shot. People say we've had crooked senators and county executives, terrorists hiding in our towns, and now we have murder to eliminate people who don't like other people's ideas. This has to stop, here and now."

There was still no response expected of Dominique or Ryan, but Dominique sensed the tirade was winding down. "We'll find whoever did this," she promised.

"Why don't you just get Mrs. Whatshername down here right now," Jaeger said. "Let's skip the pretense that the police around here can solve a murder without her."

Dominique knew it was time to keep her mouth shut again. Ryan, however, didn't get Jaeger's heavy sarcasm and blurted, "Mrs. Morris just got lucky, sir. We would have caught the murderer anyway."

Dominique cringed. The reference to the murder of a local hairdresser the year before and the inability of the police to find the murderer was still a sore point for many on the police force.

Jaeger's red face indicated the situation had gone from severe to critical. "And exactly when would that have been?"

Chastened, Ryan sealed his lips. His handsome but freckled face was pink, making an unpleasant contrast with his bright red hair.

Dominique crossed her long legs and looked from one man to the other, longing for the sanity Elliot's presence would have lent. She leaned forward and placed her hand on Jaeger's desk, itching to get her fingers on the file he had there. She knew it was about the murder of Keith Hollis and she had been up to the quarry while the site was searched and processed, but she couldn't wait to see the lab reports. The county crime scene investigators were thorough and she knew that Detective Davis, as chief investigator for the prosecutor's office, already had all this information. He and Dominique did not get along well. The man had an attitude toward her, and, in his words on one of his more malevolent days, had actually said, "You're a beautiful black woman. Why don't you go be a model instead of trying to do this work?" She hated Davis having a leg up on the town police in the present situation, especially since he was not one to share information willingly.

Jaeger practically shoved the file at her. "We don't know if he stayed in the park during the fireworks, which ended at 9:40 P.M., or if he left before they started, so we're saying that the time of death is between 8:30, when he was last seen, and midnight. We didn't find a car and assuming he wasn't killed just after leaving the park and brought up to the top of the hill, you'd have to figure the time of death was closer to 8:45 at the earliest. Maybe later if he walked. He apparently hadn't eaten, so we can't narrow it down by stomach contents."

Inside the file Dominique saw there was other information. "He had a broken neck as well as numerous head injuries. It doesn't look like he had a chance to fight back against the person who killed him. There were no defensive wounds and nothing under his fingernails."

"Could he have sustained those injuries to his head from falling?" Ryan asked. "Is it possible he wasn't pushed in, but just fell?"

"Maybe he jumped in, to avoid causing any trouble," said Jaeger sarcastically.

His tone wasn't lost on Ryan. "I just meant, why are they so sure he was murdered? He could have fallen. Maybe it was an accident. Maybe no one else was even around."

Dominique stiffened, waiting for the explosion. "Do you think we are all idiots?" Jaeger shouted. "That we can't tell an accident from a murder?"

"From what I understand," said Dominique in a soft voice so that the two men in the room would have to be quiet in order to hear her, which, with any luck, would calm them down, "there is a probability that several of those blows to the head were not made as he fell. That's also the case with some of the bruises on his arms, as if someone might have been grabbing him. The backs of his heels were scuffed, indicating he may have been dragged to the edge. We're trying to find a possible weapon. It wasn't an accident."

Jaeger's satisfied smirk at Ryan was better than his

yelling, so Dominique felt some triumph. If only Ryan would keep quiet now, they might still be partners at the end of the day. He really wasn't a bad detective, although he sometimes had to redo what he should have done differently in the first place. And Dominique wasn't ready to give up on him.

"That's right," said Jaeger, in a semi-reasonable tone. "He could not have slipped, even though the edge of the cliff is worn away over where he would have been standing."

"There is a lot of erosion at the back of the Ferrys' property," Dominique agreed. "Yet from what I saw and as you'll see in these photographs, there are no scratches on the body and no sign of anyone slipping, or grasping at rocks or branches. Hollis cleared all of that on his way down."

"There are no distinguishable footprints?" Jaeger asked in disbelief. "Are you sure the area was combed?"

"Yes, sir."

Ryan had stopped squirming and was peering over Dominique's shoulder at the folder. "It has been very dry for weeks," he said. "The last rain was over two weeks ago. The ground is rock hard."

Dominique worried that Jaeger was going to start screaming again about how he didn't need a weather report. But he didn't.

"The problem is," Dominique said, regretfully, "that the fencing contractor's crew was working for several hours before we stopped them. Any evidence was destroyed."

"Perfect." Jaeger shook his head. "I want to know every detail of every minute of the last twenty-four hours of Hollis's life. No, make that forty-eight. And I want you two to stay close to Davis and the rest of the county investigators." He stood up. "Don't forget to ask for help if you need it."

After they had left his office, Dominique was still wondering exactly who Jaeger had meant when he said ask for help. She was sure he wasn't serious about asking Wally Morris. Elliot, Mrs. Morris's new son-in-law and Dominique's former partner, who was now an assistant prosecutor for the county and the most likely other candidate to assist in the investigation, was still on his honeymoon. Neither one seemed to be someone who could help them with this case.

But maybe that wasn't true. Mrs. Morris had her finger on the pulse of Grosvenor. From what several witnesses had said so far, the victim was a controversial character in the town. Dominique, who lived in the next town, which had its own political intrigues, knew Keith Hollis was trying to develop the quarry and that there was a lot of opposition, but she hadn't paid enough attention to the proposals to know why. Mrs. Morris might know. At least it was a place to start.

Wally wiped her face with her towel before putting her tennis racket back in its bag. "You mopped the court with me today," she said to her friend.

Louise laughed. "You'll beat me next time. I had an unfair advantage."

"You mean those nine extra inches you have over me?"

"No. I meant I got to practice in Florida during the winter while you slogged through snow."

"You're not the only one who goes on vacations," Wally said.

"True. And when I came back from mine you said you were going away, but yet you're still here."

"As Nate told the Frieds last night, we're working on it. We'll go at the end of the summer. We are awaiting the birth of a second grandchild, you know. How could we leave any sooner?"

"Okay, fine. But why won't you tell me where you are going?"

Wally looked at her, putting on a mysterious face. "If I told you, I'd have to kill you."

The joke fell flat when both women remembered the news they had heard that morning. Keith Hollis had been murdered up at the quarry, or at least that was what the news media claimed. It was so sad. The three children, two of them teenagers who had been in Wally's nursery school class, and a preschooler, had all lost their father. And the circumstances of his death were so awful. Wally's knees felt weak at the very thought of how Keith fell all that way. She was never good with heights under the best of circumstances and shivers ran through her.

"I feel so awful for those girls," she said, rubbing her arms to make her goose bumps go away.

Louise nodded. "I've been trying all afternoon to figure out what I can do for Fiona and her mother."

"Who?"

"Fiona Trinity—you know, she works for Norman at the pharmacy. Her mother, Peggy, is, I mean was, Keith's sister."

"You're right," said Wally. "We have to do something. You take care of the Trinitys and I'll see what I can do for Keith's twins and their mother."

Louise nodded. "Okay, but can we spend a few minutes at the pool?"

"Twenty laps?"

"You're on."

They finished packing up their tennis gear and walked over to the town pool. But once there, they found that the murder was on everyone's lips and everyone had an opinion. Wally never even got a toe into the water.

There was a message on Wally's machine when she got out of the shower. It was from Dominique and Wally quickly returned the call.

"I was wondering if you'd do me a favor," Dominique said.

"Sure, what is it?"

"Captain Jaeger suggested I call you to get a feel for what was going on. Do you know anything about Keith Hollis?"

"Between the quarry business and the town gossip I've heard, I know quite a bit. I just don't know what you're after." Wally sighed. "I knew his daughters. I was just at their house, dropping off a little care package."

"Do you know anything about their father?"

Wally wondered what she knew that was most important to tell Dominique. She took a stab. "You are aware of Keith's marital history, aren't you? My friend Louise told me that he was working on his second divorce." It had turned out that Louise had some information on the subject, because the sale of the Hollises' house was a major factor in the split. Tori filed for divorce soon after Keith contracted to sell the house and all its contents without her knowledge, to finance his venture, so the story went, even though Tori was dead set against it. Unfortunately for her, the house was titled only in Keith's name. She was only living in the house until all the papers were signed, then she'd have to move. In addition, Keith had taken his teenage daughters' college funds and used them for his new project, as well.

"My partner Ryan is getting the background work on Mr. Hollis started," Dominique said. "I wanted to get your impression."

Wally thought about it. "Maybe I could help. Do you want me to come over there?"

"Definitely not," said Dominique. "The air conditioner went down again a half hour ago. Is it okay if I come to your house?"

"Sure," Wally said. "I'll make us some iced tea."

It didn't take long for Dominique to drive the mile and a half from the police station. She pulled her car far up into Wally's driveway, about halfway between the back of the house and the barn where Wally's husband, Nate, had his investment and insurance businesses.

"Move out of the way, Sammy," Wally said to her black Labrador retriever. "Let Dominique in before you cover her in kisses."

The police detective greeted the dog and came into the kitchen. She had always liked the room with its oak cabinets and terra cotta floor. Wally's kitchen was a warm, friendly place, full of delicious food generously shared as well as interesting, kind people.

Wally was as good as her word. She had a tall glass of iced tea waiting for Dominique along with some homemade blueberry muffins. "I see you have more time on your hands."

Wally laughed. "You are a good detective, aren't you? I have some extra time during the summer, since there isn't as much to prepare for my class. Believe me, I'm enjoying every minute of my leisure time."

"I hope you won't hate me then," Dominique said. "I'm asking you to get involved in the case, at least a bit. The only town-wide discussion I'd heard about was that big competition for the museum of nineteenth century stuff."

Wally nodded. There were posters all over town for keeping Grosvenor clean and friendly. The old mansion that people were hoping to convert into the Hampton museum was pictured with a caption telling the people of the town they could make it happen.

"Now," said Dominique, "I hear there is some big controversy about something else. Can you tell me about the quarry and the fighting?"

Wally sat down in the chair opposite Dominique and

opened a folder. "This is some of the literature put out by the various factions." She laid out the collection of flyers into separate piles.

Dominique was impressed with Wally's organization. But, she reflected as she went through the papers, a nursery school teacher would have to be organized or she wouldn't survive. That was probably a factor in how Wally was able to help the police in the past, that and her ability to get people to talk. Some might say she was a busybody, but actually she was just a good listener and very smart.

Some of Wally's acuity had led Dominique and her partners, Elliot and Ryan, straight to solving cases. But Wally's persistence had, in some instances, caused Dominique to work so much overtime that she barely saw her own husband, James. Wally and Nate had become patients in James's dentistry practice and they got along well with him, now. He had even forgiven Wally for those broken dates caused by her insistence on immediate investigation of every idea she had.

"There is one group," Wally said, "against the quarry because it would increase the population of the school district without increasing the tax revenues sufficiently to cover the new students. There is even a possibility that a new school would have to be built, something the town has been trying to avoid for years." She patted the appropriate pile. Dire warnings about overcrowded classrooms were emblazoned on the front.

"Another group is comprised of people, such as Professor Ferry, who live on the rim of the quarry and would lose their wildlife vistas. By the way, I don't know if you know that Gabe Ferry is running, or I guess I should say was, against Keith for the open town council position."

"I did hear that," Dominique said. She and Ryan had both wondered if that could possibly be a factor in the case.

Wally handed her another flyer. "This is from the homeowners on the one street leading out of the quarry, the one at the bottom, who would have to put up with the extra traffic. They've recently joined forces with the first group of homeowners on an environmental impact platform." She wrinkled her nose. "The only thing is, they are not really the environmentalists. That is this crowd." Wally pulled over a much bigger stack of material. "This is Nate's group. They've done studies, and there really could be flooding issues, as well as a loss of habitat for many species who have made their home up there since the quarry closed. It would also mean less open space, which New Jersey is trying to maintain." She pointed to another handout. "This is the pro set, at least the recognized one. They are pro-development because it would mean increased revenue and traffic in the local stores."

"What is this other bunch?" Dominique asked.

"The fringe, miscellaneous factions, some pro, some con. There are people who believe ghosts in there will be released if the land is cleared. Some others are so far from reality that all I can do is wonder if they don't have something better to do with their lives."

Dominique was surprised at Wally's criticism. It was quite unlike her. "I'm not sure I understand," she said.

"I don't know if you've been following the local newspaper," Wally said. She pulled out a copy of what turned out to be the most recent issue and opened it to the editorial page. "There is another letter in there from Kelley Peren complaining about the fences around the top of the quarry."

"Who?" Dominique said.

"Oh, maybe you don't know about this. Kelley Peren is a graphic artist who lives in town. She's the woman who nearly fell into the quarry last winter when she went looking for her cat. The cat had run out of the house and Kelley went after it. It got into a tree on the edge of the quarry," Wally said, before pausing to swallow hard, giving Dominique the impression that the concept was frightening to Wally, "and Kelley decided she couldn't wait for the cat to come down, so she went to get her. She lost her footing and ended up hanging from the tree by the hood of her jacket."

Wally went on. "The homeowners came home and found the cat taking a bath in a spot of sunshine and Kelley suspended dangerously close to the unprotected edge of the quarry. She sued them and has been waging a campaign to get all the homeowners on the rim to put up contiguous safety fences. Keith took up her cause and said, in one of his campaign flyers, that he is going to push for an ordinance to get all the homeowners up there to erect a certain type of very expensive fence, if they don't already have a safety fence."

Although Dominique had heard about a woman nearly falling into the quarry, she didn't quite see why that mattered and said so.

"Because," Wally said, her voice rising with each word, "people have been scrambling to put up some kind of fence ahead of any such ordinance, reasoning that the cheaper ones can be grandfathered in, even if they don't meet the new requirements. So many fences are down for repairs now. Maybe that's how Keith was able to fall into the quarry."

"He didn't fall in. He was pushed or thrown in."

Wally paled and bit her lip. "Oh. So the news was actually right. But maybe it wouldn't have happened if there had been a sturdy six-foot fence. Maybe Kelley was right."

"Are you saying that the murder was related to Kelley Peren's letter? But that just got published."

"Oh, no," said Wally. "I'm sorry I wasn't clear. There have been many letters. For a while they were in the paper every week. This has been going on since late autumn. The whole safety issue that she raised was one of the reasons the town council went along with allowing the proposed building in the quarry. They'd rather have taxes on land that someone else owns than lawsuits against their own property any day. The land, which is wild and has wetlands, is not the safest place in the world, so those council members who wanted to buy the land for a park were overruled."

Dominique saw her point. It was something to consider when they were asking questions. "I'm guessing you don't want to go up to the quarry with me and have a peek in," she said.

"Heaven forbid. I'm not one for heights. Unless you think it's really important?" Her eyes looked worried.

"No. By the way," she said, "just out of curiosity, what little care package did you bring Merle Hollis and her daughters?" For as long as Dominique had known her, Wally always brought food to families in distress, usually something wonderful.

Wally frowned. "All I could manage today was a barbequed chicken, some salad ingredients, a bread and a cake. But I'll see what I can do for them in the next few days."

Dominique wasn't surprised. Her friend might not be able to look into a really big hole in the ground, but she could always take care of people.

Chapter Three

Dominique rapped impatiently on her desk early Monday morning. "Ryan, we have to get going."

"I'll be right there," he said. He turned back to the phone he'd been speaking on and lowered his voice so much that Dominique wasn't sure the person he was speaking to could even hear him. Crystal. His girlfriend.

When Ryan first started dating Crystal, the receptionist at the fanciest hair salon in Grosvenor, Dominique was immediately impressed by how much more mature he had become. He went from just being a pretty-faced, muscular, wannabe detective destined to flop at his first post to a guy with a future. He wasn't all the way up to being the professional he needed to be, but he was getting there a lot quicker now that the savvy woman with the chalk-white makeup and improbably colored hair was part of his life. The only problem was, Ryan needed to hear her voice at least once every two hours.

"I'm ready," he said after another annoying minute. "Let's go."

The two of them drove over to a three-story house just a mile from the center of town. Like most of the houses in Grosvenor, the house had been built in the twenties.

"I don't get it," Ryan said. "Why would a guy like Hollis, who had all that money, live in a house like this?"

Dominique shook her head. "It is a far cry from the three-thousand-square-foot house he was living in last year." She filled him in on the sale of the house and the pending divorce. "He had to move somewhere when he and his wife split up and I guess he was being frugal."

"But didn't he make a pile of cash on the house?"

"Not yet. Since it hasn't closed all he got was the collateral capital he needed for his bank loans. It enabled him to get a bridge loan to cover the gap."

Ryan shook his head. "So he bought this instead?"

"No, he doesn't own this. It belongs to a friend of his. Hollis was staying here while he got his affairs in order."

"With a woman?"

"Did you get that idea from Crystal?" Dominique asked. Lately Crystal had been playing amateur detective on Ryan's investigations, which, until Hollis's murder, had mainly consisted of break-ins and car and bicycle thefts. So far, while Crystal had sound ideas, she hadn't managed to solve anything. Her failures, though, didn't stop her from trying.

Dominique suspected that Crystal had been influenced by her encounters with Wally Morris. In fact, the salon receptionist had been useful in the investigation centered there. Ryan and Dominique were now on the biggest case since that one and it looked as if Crystal was ready to roll up her sleeves to dig in.

"She might have suggested that Hollis was killed because he cheated on his wife."

"Does she know for sure he was cheating on Mrs. Hollis?"

"No, I don't think so."

Dominique resisted the urge to take Ryan's shoulders in her hands and shake him. Even if the cheating were a possibility, it didn't seem to be relevant to the house they were about to investigate. "If there was a woman, she didn't live here," Dominique said. "This house is owned by a man named Ron Walsh."

Since Walsh was not home, the detectives split up and started canvassing the houses nearby. Most of their attempts went unanswered, and they left their business cards at those addresses, but in one house, a woman came to the door.

She was about sixty and several small children accompanied her to the door. In the background a television was playing and Dominique thought she heard the familiar closing theme to *All My Children,* one of her grandmother's favorite soap operas.

At Ryan's request, the woman gave her name, Georgia Dewey, and occupation, day care provider. She invited them in.

Every square inch of floor was covered with toys and

several infants squirmed among them, oblivious to the visitors. The older children, some with faces that looked as if they had just had some of the Chef Boyardee that Dominique's nose told her had been lunch, peered curiously at Dominique and Ryan. Their empty bowls were strewn over the coffee table along with half-empty glasses of apple juice and wadded up dirty paper towels. One child, whose face bore tear stains, looked at the detectives fearfully.

"That house?" said Georgia, once Dominique explained the reason for their visit. She didn't stop what she was doing, which turned out to be cleaning the rest of the children's faces and straightening up, "I think they're some kind of gay brothel." She had the sense to lower her voice when she said this, but it didn't stop some of the children hearing. Dominique wondered what their parents would have to say about their brand new word, brothel.

"What makes you think so, ma'am?" she asked.

"They come and go all day and all night long over there."

"Do you know who they are?"

"Well, your murder victim, for one. And Ronny, the man who owns the house. I thought he was a nice person until he took up with all those men." She picked up a tray full of bowls, spoons, and cups and took them into the kitchen. Dominique followed.

"There are others?"

"Yeah, two or three at least. Only one there now, besides Ronny, now that Hollis took that swan dive."

Dominique suspected, based on her choice of words,

that after the children went home for the day, Mrs. Dewey turned the television over to *Law and Order* re-runs. The television channel had been changed to PBS at two o'clock, and the children were all engrossed. There was a window for Dominique and Ryan to ask questions, at least until one of the babies cried.

"Do you know the man's name?" Ryan asked.

"As a matter of fact I do. I know practically all the names, since the substitute mailman around here doesn't look too closely when he sorts the mail. Let me see, there've been letters here for Keith Hollis, and Ronny, of course, and also Norville Morgan, and Randolph Quaker, Izmir something or other, and one other, but I can't remember his name."

They thanked Georgia and asked her to call if she remembered anything else. By the time they left, Dominique was more than a little relieved to get outside to the fresh air as at least one of the babies had needed changing.

"Let's go check out these men," she said.

Monday morning, when Wally got to the synagogue where she taught nursery school, she had to thread her way past several construction vehicles and around a huge trash container overflowing with demolished wall board and cabinets. She found the last possible parking space and pulled her car into it.

There was a half hour before the car pool lines would start and due to the situation with the construction, no parents were being allowed to park and take their children inside. The teachers would form a line, take the children out of each car, and hand each one on to the next teacher until the children were all inside. That was the only way they could make sure everyone would be safe and accounted for. It was something of a water brigade, with children being the commodity moved along the line.

The problems continued once everyone was inside, however, since the work was being done on the nursery wing and all the summer classes were being held on the Hebrew school level, upstairs. This meant a lot of walking up and down past the heavily plastic-curtained first floor.

Abby, the director, had tried unsuccessfully to cancel the summer session but the board of directors of both the school and the synagogue had been unwilling to inconvenience either the parents of the student/campers, who had been counting on attending this summer, or the budget. That decision had only served to make normally irritable, nervous, hyperactive Abby more difficult to deal with. She had refused to be in charge of the renovations to the nursery school until the board suggested that maybe they would hire someone else to take over for the summer. The thought of that had apparently made her decide to take on the project herself, causing everyone else nothing but additional stress, as she was a complete control freak.

"You'd better hurry," Abby said. "Those children will be here soon and we can't risk anything happening to them. The board should have understood that, but, no, they wouldn't listen to me."

Wally briefly imagined that she had been listening to a tape recording, because it seemed to be what Abby had said, verbatim, every morning that the summer school had been in session.

"I think we'll try it another way," Abby said, also echoing her daily routine. They had moved the children in through the synagogue entrance, the Hebrew school doors, and the delivery entry for the kitchens. Each method had gone smoothly and it didn't seem to matter which they used. But that didn't stop Abby from trying to find the perfect way of entering the building. "I think we'll bring them in through the playground access."

"Won't that bring them right into the construction area?" Wally asked.

Abby stared at her, blinking her eyes as if someone had thrown water in them. "Oh, maybe you're right. We'll do what we did last week."

There had been three different methods that week, Wally thought, and only three because the other two days they had been off for the holiday. She had no idea which one Abby was intending to use. But she figured she'd find out and it was time to line up for the cars.

Minivans, SUVs, a few station wagons, and one odd sedan with a father in it lined up in the driveway of the synagogue. All of them seemed to wait patiently for their charges to be collected, but by the time the process was over, Wally was looking for some fresh air, free from exhaust fumes. That wasn't forthcoming because the July morning was as humid as they came.

Abby was waving her arms, directing the line of children up the stairs to the Hebrew school classrooms.

In contrast to the brightly lit and colorful nursery class-rooms, before their demolition, that is, these rooms were drab and dark. The chairs were too large for the little children and the worktables too high. Abby hadn't foreseen the problem and had donated the furniture in the nursery rooms to a needy school in Newark before the new equipment arrived. To be fair, Wally admitted to herself, they had been promised delivery of the new furniture in May, but had been warned there might be a back order problem. It turned out to be one of many problems.

The phone in the Hebrew school office rang and Abby went to answer it. As there were no Hebrew classes in the summer, it was likely a parent calling to say her little camper would be absent. With relief that Abby was out of the way, Wally separated her campers from the group and brought them into what was serving as her classroom for the summer. Although Wally had done her best to fill it with craft supplies, books, and music, the old computers had gone the way of the furniture and the new ones could not be used until the nursery wing was in compliance with the new electrical code. Still, Wally was a pro, and confident she could keep the children happy.

The children had finished their work on their tissue paper collages and had already gone home for the day when Abby came into the room. She had an exasperated look on her face and motioned Wally to come to the door.

"I don't have time to deal with that man," she said,

explaining that the contractor was on the phone but that she had an appointment. "He doesn't seem to understand plain English and wants to go over every instruction I give him. You'll have to talk to him."

That was the last thing Wally wanted to do and she knew she was taking a big risk. If something happened and the renovations deviated in the slightest from whatever vision Abby had, Wally would never hear the end of it. She went to the office, picked up the phone, and listened to five minutes of his complaints about Abby and one minute of his explanation of what he wanted to do with the wiring for the computer area in the first place.

"That sounds fine," Wally said, wondering what all the fuss was about. "That's the way the computer corner makes the most sense."

"Not according to your director."

Wally felt a sinking sensation in her stomach. What had she just agreed to that Abby didn't want? "I beg your pardon?"

"She wanted them in a line, not in a semi-circle. It would have meant much more wire and less room for the other things she wants." He went on at length to convince her that he was right. Wally began to see Abby's point about the man's need to restate every detail.

"I'll explain that to her," Wally promised. "Is there anything else?"

There was a low chuckle on the line. "Is there any way I can deal with you instead of her?"

"She's the director. And she's in charge."

"All right," said the contractor. "Too bad."

She left a note telling Abby it was all straightened out. Sooner or later Abby would find out what Wally had agreed to and Wally would have to justify it. Already it was looking like a less-than-peachy day.

Wally watched Nate. He wasn't doing anything particularly interesting, just reading the newspaper, but somehow Wally felt she had to watch him, to wait for a good moment to raise her concerns.

Naturally, he asked what she was doing.

"Nothing," she said.

His left eyebrow went up. "Oh, really?"

"Absolutely."

She looked at her watch and at Nate again.

"Is there something on your mind?"

"Not really."

"Then why are you watching me?"

Wally sighed. "It's just that there was supposed to be a meeting tonight. But it was called off because Keith Hollis is dead."

"Yes. Does something not make sense to you about calling off the meeting protesting the development of the quarry that won't be developed now because the developer is dead?"

"Well, no. It does make sense."

"Then what's wrong?"

"It just seems so weird. As if something should be said but hasn't been. Instead of people just saying, oh well, it isn't an issue anymore, let's just not worry about it anymore."

Nate leaned forward and, taking Wally's hand, brought her to sit with him on the sofa. "That may be how it looks," he explained, "but there's much more to it. First, the members decided to skip tonight's meeting out of consideration for the family. They didn't want to appear to be celebrating. There will be other meetings, though, because another developer could come try to do the same thing."

The windows were all open since a passing thunderstorm had substantially lowered the temperature. The sound of crickets and other people's air conditioners kept the air humming. Wally leaned against Nate and relaxed. "Oh."

"Oh? Is that all you have to say? You were looking at me as if I was some kind of unfeeling monster, and now you say 'Oh?' "

"Sorry."

"Do you want to make it up to me?"

"I suppose." She sat up. "What did you have in mind?"

"I could think of a few things," he said, grinning suggestively. "But I was wondering if you'd like to go to the funeral with me."

"You're going to Keith Hollis's funeral? I would think that was the last thing you'd want to do. You hated the man."

"Don't be silly. I didn't know him. I didn't like what he wanted to do and I thought it was selfish and greedy, but I didn't really care about him one way or another. Still, I think we should go to the funeral."

Wally pulled herself away from her husband's embrace. "I was thinking of going anyway," she said. "For his daughters, to show support. But I haven't been able to arrange for a substitute to cover my class. I'll go do that right now."

Nate held his arms wide open. "I'll be waiting."

Chapter Four

Wally and Nate drove up about fifteen minutes early to the church where the funeral was being held. They had taken care to dress suitably, even though it was quite warm out. Wally wore a two-piece gray-and-white dress and Nate wore a black sports jacket and gray slacks. She quickly noticed there were a lot of people there and many had different ideas of what to wear for the occasion. It seemed to Wally that everyone in town involved in the quarry dispute showed up.

Soon after they arrived, Wally saw Gabriel Ferry drive up with his wife, Petra. Wally studied his face for a minute. He was a beloved history professor because he had a way of making history come alive and also had a great sense of humor. Wally's friend Louise had taken to calling him Indiana Jones, since he was handsome, well built, and charismatic. He was smart too, and his books had received good critical reviews. Wally realized that some people might think that Gabe had several reasons to want Keith Hollis out of the picture. They were opponents both in their stances on the quarry and in politics, each running for the same town council seat. It had been too early to predict which way the election would go, and now no one would ever know.

Nate inclined his head toward Gabe, who was wearing an ivory linen bush jacket, and Petra, who wore a muted version of her usual somewhat hippie wardrobe. She, too, was a professor, but she taught English, mostly to freshmen. Wally loved hearing about the fractured sentences Petra found when she graded papers.

The Morrises and the Ferrys had been friendly for years and saw each other socially. Gabe opposed the building in the quarry because his house overlooked the pit and his view would have been radically changed by having a development beneath him, while Nate opposed the building in the quarry for environmental reasons. Gabe's whole platform for running for town council stressed the importance of maintaining property values while still preserving the charm of the small village.

A large group of people mounted the church steps and walked past Wally. She recognized a few of them and knew that one of the women was Keith's campaign treasurer, at least according to the literature she'd received almost weekly. Her husband was also listed on the campaign flyers, but Wally couldn't remember in what capacity. The whole group seemed shell-shocked as they walked inside the church. Whatever people said about Keith, he had his followers, Wally knew, and they were loyal.

A few minutes later, Louise came to stand next to her. Louise's red hair spilled out from beneath her broad-brimmed, black mesh hat and onto the shoulders of the long black jumper she wore with a white T-shirt. "I see everyone who is anyone is here," she said, watching people enter the church.

"Norman isn't," Wally observed.

"He had to stay at the pharmacy," Louise explained, "since Fiona is Keith Hollis's niece and naturally had to be here."

Bucky Ralston, the former owner of the quarry which was now causing so much talk, walked up the steps with his wife, Gretchen. He was wearing a seersucker suit, red bow tie, and white buck shoes, and Gretchen wore a navy suit and matching pumps, along with a string of pearls. They didn't stop to chat. Wally knew both of them, having worked on a committee with Gretchen, but she and Nate did not travel in the country club set as the Ralstons did. They were about ten years older than the Morrises, and Gretchen had a town pedigree dating back several generations.

"If only Bucky hadn't agreed to sell the quarry to Keith," said Louise, "this whole thing wouldn't have happened."

Wally looked at her friend. "Do you really believe Keith's plans for the quarry brought about his murder?"

Louise shrugged. "You're the detective, not I."

"I think we should go inside," said Nate, ushering

Wally up the steps with Louise trailing behind. They stepped out of the bright sunshine into the chilled air of the beautiful Catholic church and found their places in the pews. Wally just had time to notice that Dominique and her partner were in the back before Keith Hollis's family walked in.

Wally looked at Keith Hollis's twin daughters as they walked with their mother, Merle. Lara and Amber were identical and had been good friends of one of Wally's friend's daughters, also a recent Grosvenor High School grad. Amber, Wally had heard, was set to go to Franklin and Marshall, and Lara was going to NYU, both expensive schools, and if their college funds had really been emptied, they might need to defer attending.

About halfway through the service, after the procession had worked its way to the front of the church and the initial prayers, various readings, and gospel had been read, the priest took his place at the lectern for the homily. In just a few sentences it became clear that it was going to be hard for this man to speak well of the dead.

"He gave to charity," the priest said, "and he made no distinction between people." People shifted uncomfortably and several people coughed.

The priest continued. "He had high hopes for our community and he was a lover of the arts."

There was more squirming. Wally wasn't sure if it was based on the simple way that the priest made the statements, not citing examples, or on people in the church privately disagreeing with the priest's words.

Nothing was said about him as a father, or husband,

or uncle, or brother. The priest's remarks were reminiscent of Mark Anthony's statement that he had come to bury Caesar, not to praise him.

It seemed to Wally that the priest was having difficulty finding anything else comforting to say about Keith Hollis. Sometimes at funerals awkward eulogies resulted from speakers not knowing the deceased, but Wally had the distinct impression from her visit with Merle that this speaker was familiar with Keith and his personality. The priest had just left a few moments before Wally arrived with her care package on Friday. Merle gave Wally the sense that the priest had also counseled the family after Keith moved out.

She looked at Merle Hollis, Keith's first wife and mother of his twins. Although dressed in black just as the rest of the immediate family was, she remained dry-eyed as far as Wally could tell, almost stoically. But she sat on the pew close to her daughters, as if to give them strength. They both seemed to need it; the identical girls cried the same way. Wally choked up just looking at their grief.

Tori Hollis, Keith's second wife, sat across the aisle with her daughter. The term trophy wife, with regard to Tori, had come readily to several people's lips at the pool the other day. Tori's strutting around the town pool incensed the women and amused the men. Louise screamed for two days about one gold lamé bathing suit Tori had worn. "Who does she think she is, Pamela Anderson?"

But even though there had clearly been medical enhancement of Tori's attributes, she was reported to be a nice woman, if somewhat caught up in material things. And from what Wally could see, she was only in her late twenties, though Keith had been forty-five, according to the newspaper.

"Let us pray," said the priest when he had concluded his attempts to speak well of the dead. Everyone bowed his head and there was silence.

A moment later a woman a few years older than Keith took the lectern. Wally had noticed the woman sitting next to Fiona and a few other people and surmised she was Keith's sister, Peggy. They didn't seem to resemble each other, but then again, Wally's own children didn't look that much like him.

"My brother was a good man," Peggy said, with obvious difficulty. She paused, letting that sit with the attendees, as if hoping that her words would somehow change the opinions of the mourners.

"I saw a different side of Keith. He was a good son and a good brother. Most of you don't know this, but Keith gave me a priceless gift—one of his kidneys. Without it, I would have died. It was a courageous thing for a seventeen-year-old to do and it meant he had to give up football and his chances for a scholarship. He did that for me." Her voice cracked, and she paused a moment before continuing.

"I know some of you may have been angry with Keith over the years, but he harbored no ill will toward any of you. There was no need to . . ." She burst into tears and could not go on. A man who had been sitting nearby helped her return to her seat.

When Fiona wrapped her arms around her sobbing

mother, Wally, through her own tears, saw tears in Louise's eyes.

No one else chose to speak. Closing prayers lasted fifteen minutes and finally the casket was removed to the hearse for its trip to the cemetery.

Out in the bright sunshine a line of cars was forming for the trip to the cemetery. Wally's little group would not be joining them but they watched as the people moved into position. Most of the people who had sat at the front of the church maneuvered their cars behind the hearse and limousine where the immediate family waited.

Many of the cars were late model SUVs or luxury cars. Wally could practically see Nate drool over a few of the sports cars. While he was looking at one of them, a silver Audi TT convertible with a smiling man at the wheel, she gave him a poke. "Your tongue is hanging out."

"I wouldn't wear that cap though," Nate said, half to himself. What he had against it, Wally couldn't figure out.

"It's better than getting a sunburn," Louise said, pulling her own hat lower over her face.

"Would you two like to join me for lunch?" Nate asked when the cortege moved away.

"You're on," said Louise as she took him by the arm. Wally trotted along with them, trying her best to keep up with her companions.

They chose a seat far in the back of one of the more upscale restaurants in town—several cuts above the places where Wally and Louise usually went for lunch.

Then again, they were dressed somewhat better than usual, so they didn't feel out of place.

"Why do you suppose there was so much fidgeting while the priest spoke?" Wally asked after the waiter had taken their drink and lunch orders.

Louise frowned. "There's been a lot of talk."

Nate raised an eyebrow.

"For example," Louise said, "when the priest said that Keith made no distinction between people, some might have been of the opinion that he was right—Keith was rude to everyone."

"Did you ever talk to him?"

"Yes, Nate, I did. It wasn't fun. He essentially told us, the group of real estate agents who were asking about his plans for selling his new properties, that he wouldn't deal with such airheads in a million years." She paused while the waiter served white wine to the women and an iced tea to Nate.

Louise took a sip of her wine. "And look how he treated his wife."

"Merle or Tori?" said Wally, after tasting her own.

"Tori. I heard there was a pre-nup."

"Where did you hear that?"

"One of my clients is a friend of hers. She said that since Tori never really had a chance to establish herself in business before she got married and became a lady of leisure, she made him sign an agreement."

"Who said she couldn't work after she got married?" Wally asked.

"Supposedly Keith. He said she could be more of an

asset to him if she was available all the time. That's why they had a full-time nanny until they split up."

"In what way could she be an asset?"

"Lunch," Louise said. "And bridge, golf, tennis, whatever a potential investor's wife was into. Keith would woo the husband and Tori would entertain the wife. That's why he married her."

Nate narrowed his eyes and stared at Louise. "As opposed to . . . ?"

She laughed. "I've always said you were shrewd, Nate. Yes, she may not have been his first choice. But the other applicant, so to speak, was not in Tori's class, and that's what Keith needed."

Wally sputtered. "Other applicant?"

"Alberta Dellaquan. He had been mixed up with her before."

So Wally had heard—from Merle.

Louise continued. "Did you know that Merle first found out about it after Keith cashed a check at the construction company and Alberta wrote on the back, 'Did you know that your husband is sleeping with the daughter of the owner?' "

Nate sputtered. "You learned all this from your client?"

Louise couldn't answer because just then their lunches were served. Wally and Louise had ordered pasta primavera and Nate the penne with a light pomodoro sauce. Nate waited a moment before digging in. "The whole thing about Tori being a bigger asset than that other woman? Was that why he divorced Merle?"

"Oh, I think there were many reasons. But yes. She said Merle wasn't the type to woo people's wives."

Wally felt her blood begin to boil and she stabbed into a piece of broccoli. "Is that because she had a real job teaching high school English?"

Nate put his hand on Wally's arm. "Calm down, sweetheart. The rest of us appreciate teachers."

"It's not such a surprise that someone killed him, is it?" Louise said, eating a bite of carrot. "Look how he treated people."

"But he gave his sister his kidney," Wally pointed out. "That was a big sacrifice."

Louise shook her head. "Let's put it this way. It was a good deed that he exploited by making it appear as if his sister should pay him back for it her whole life."

"What do you mean?"

"She put him through college. His parents were gone, so Peggy paid, at least until he dropped out and went to work for the Dellaquan Brothers and started making all that money. But before that, Peggy worked two jobs, even when Fiona was little. That's probably why her husband's eyes wandered."

"That's your whole case? That proves he was making her pay her whole life?"

"I may have exaggerated a bit," Louise admitted. "But just look at how Keith lived and how his sister is still struggling."

Wally would have to take Louise's word for it, since she didn't know Peggy personally. It might be a good idea to learn more about her, if she could. "Who was that sitting next to her at the funeral, the man she was leaning on? Are he and Peggy seeing each other?"

Louise toyed with her linguine for a minute. "I didn't think she was seeing anyone. I think he's just a friend of the family."

Wally was hit with another wave of sadness. She knew that Peggy was truly grieving over her brother, and Wally had to wonder who else was, besides his children. She was willing to bet there weren't many.

Chapter Five

"**D**id you have a chance to check out Mr. Quaker?" Dominique asked Ryan, who was half sitting on his desk.

He struck his usual pose, one hand on his hip and the other holding his notebook out. Every time Dominique saw that she had an urge to sing "I'm a little teapot." Ryan also had a habit of gazing down onto the notepad as if he had to get closer to see it, giving him a somewhat hunched appearance that made Dominique want to tell him to sit up straight. Even after a year and a half, her new partner took some getting used to.

But he had done his homework on the residents of the house across the street from Georgia Dewey, the one that had all the "strange goings-on."

"Mr. Quaker is a former house guest of Ron Walsh. He is an engineer working in the Princeton area now and has a house there. While he was residing here in Grosvenor, he was going through a divorce and unemployed."

"Did Keith Hollis live there while Mr. Quaker was there?"

"No. Quaker had been gone for at least six months. He didn't know Mr. Hollis."

"Did either of the other people Mrs. Dewey mentioned live there at the same time as Hollis?"

Ryan flipped a page in his notebook. "Yes, both Mr. Izmir Fakhouri, although I should have said Dr. Fakhouri, and Mr. Morgan live there. It is the same story as with Mr. Quaker and I suppose the victim. They are going through divorces and staying with Mr. Walsh for the time."

"This Dr. Fakhouri," Dominique said, "where does he work?"

"Emergency at Glenside hospital."

"That's probably why he keeps what Georgia Dewey called strange hours. He probably goes into work in the evening. What about Mr. Morgan?"

"He's a high school teacher and coaches the fencing team."

"If it's anything like the fencing team at my high school," said Dominique, "then he leaves very early in the morning to coach the team before school starts, since they can't get the gym later in the day."

"I'll check it out," said Ryan.

Dominique would have thought he'd find that out at the same time, especially after what Mrs. Dewey said. But she didn't say that to Ryan. She knew he'd follow up now. "Did you get the information on Mr. Walsh?"

"Also divorced, although that was many years ago. He is an architect and he travels frequently. That was why he lets so many people stay at his house. He told me they help take care of his cat when he is away, but—"

"What?"

"I think he's just a really nice guy who is kind to his friends."

Gritting her teeth, Dominique realized Ryan had already concluded that a potential suspect was innocent, without a solid basis or alibi. But something about what he said puzzled her. Actually there were a lot of things about what he said and how he said it. She began to sense a feminine viewpoint. "How long has Crystal known Mr. Walsh?"

"All her life. Growing up she knew one of his daughters, before he got divorced, and she said he was one of the nicest dads around. She has seen him frequently since then and says he always seems interested in how she is. In fact, he knew who I was before I opened my mouth."

"I trust you verified what she and Mr. Walsh told you," Dominique said.

Ryan looked hurt. "Of course."

Dominique hurried to apologize to her sensitive partner. "Sorry. Let's continue." She looked at her own notes. "That might explain why Walsh, Fakhouri, and Morgan were all at the funeral and Quaker was not, since he moved away and didn't know the victim. What do you have for alibis for the three men?"

Ryan went back to his teapot pose. "Walsh was away with his brother for the Fourth of July weekend. They were mountain climbing." He flipped back a page. "Fakhouri was at the hospital, a twelve-hour shift starting at eight, due to the holiday. And Morgan was at the day camp where he works, supervising their Fourth of July sleep over. It is thirty miles from Grosvenor. Witnesses can account for the whole evening."

"So none of them could have done it," Dominique concluded.

"I would suppose not."

"We aren't here to suppose," said an angry voice. It belonged to Captain Jaeger and Dominique immediately wished she had a private office rather than an open cubicle.

"We aren't, sir," she said.

Ryan scurried off the desk and into his chair. "No, sir."

To Dominique's surprise, Jaeger just grunted and moved past their cubes. He didn't chew them out, or make any helpful suggestions. Apparently he was trying to follow the department psychologist's suggestions to improve his interpersonal relationships.

They had all attended the symposium run by the psychologist. Tensions in the department seemed to have decreased somewhat. Antacid use was up though, especially with Jaeger, if Dominique's observations were correct.

"We'll have to check in with Davis in a little while," Dominique reminded Ryan. "The county wants more frequent updates and Elliot isn't here to relay them."

She knew she had made a mistake mentioning that when she saw Ryan's face. How long was she going to have to put up with his sullen behavior every time her former partner's name was mentioned? It was time for this kid to grow up already. Birth order aside, even though Ryan was the youngest of thirteen children, he couldn't be a child forever.

It was good the family didn't live in Grosvenor, in Dominique's opinion. Elliot had said the same thing last year, when two of Ryan's sisters had stopped him and chastised him for being mean to their little brother. When Ryan heard about it, his face turned the color of his hair, and he made the whole family promise to stay out of his business and out of Grosvenor, showing some backbone for the first time. But he couldn't hide his feelings when Elliot's name came up.

He seemed to get over his funk and stood up, back straight. "I'll make sure we have all those details covered before we call Davis."

Crystal's influence again, Dominique guessed. She'd probably do more toward making Ryan a man than any of his myriad sisters and brothers.

Wally's youngest son, Mark, was in the kitchen when she got home from the nursery school/day camp. He was bare-chested, barefoot, and barely awake. "Aren't you feeling well?" she asked, reaching up as high as she could to feel his forehead. Her over six-foot-tall son may have been a recent Princeton graduate, but he was still her little boy.

"No, tonight is the cruise for the summer associates. I don't have to go to work today."

Once again Wally marveled at what some young people were offered these days. Mark was barely twenty-two, yet he had an incredibly lucrative summer job on Wall Street, which he'd had every summer since his first year of college, with increasing benefits, and he was starting an MBA program at Wharton in the fall. And with all that, he'd gotten the day off so he'd be fresh for the cruise around New York harbor with its fabulous food and views. Not for the first time did Wally wonder where she'd gone wrong. Being born thirty years too soon might have had something to do with it. Not having a supportive and wealthy enough family to send her to a fancy private university might have been another. And being female, back in the early years of the women's movement, probably was a factor. But Wally wasn't jealous of Mark, not any more so than of Debbie's new career as a lawyer or Rachel's psychology practice, which she juggled while raising her family. Perks were fun and Mark had earned himself quite a few. She felt only pride at what a successful and independent young man he had become and she knew she'd miss him when he moved out again, this time to Pennsylvania.

Mark went over to the refrigerator. "So what's there to eat?"

By the time Wally finished making Mark an enormous lunch to tide him over long enough to get to the cocktail hour, Nate was back from his meeting. He looked at the dirty dishes in front of his son and at Wally, who was finishing a yogurt. "He ate again? He made himself a four-egg cheese omelet two hours ago."

Wally shrugged at her husband. "What did you find out?"

Mark wiped his mouth with his napkin. "Are you two investigating Keith Hollis's murder?"

"No, of course not," said Wally. "The police are doing a fine job of that. But as concerned citizens, we are trying to find out what we can, to help the police, of course."

Nate filled two glasses with ice, poured coffee into each and gave one to Wally. "All I did was talk to Gabriel Ferry."

Wally poured some milk into her iced coffee. "What did he say?"

"Et tu brute?"

"I beg your pardon?"

Mark laughed. "I'm guessing you weren't the first person to talk to Dr. Ferry, Dad."

"I would say you're probably right," said Nate. "He's been questioned by the county as well as the town police plus his yard has been inspected by the forensics people to the point that every flower Petra planted was trampled."

Wally sniffed. "Is that any way to preserve evidence?"

Mark leaned down and kissed her on the head. "You are too much, Mom. I'm going to take a shower." He grabbed one last cookie and walked out of the room. Sammy, his black nose on the ground sniffing for fallen crumbs, trailed behind.

"What did Mark mean by that?"

Nate took a cookie from the jar. "I think he believes you are taking your investigating work too seriously."

"I'm not investigating anything," Wally said. "I

wouldn't have time anyway. Have you forgotten we have a new grandchild coming any day?"

"Not exactly any day."

"Close enough. Now would you tell me what Gabe said?"

"Okay. First of all, he was really mad at Keith for several reasons, all of which he says he explained to the police. Keith had mounted a mudslinging fundraising campaign to help fund his upcoming council election bid against Gabe."

Wally resisted the urge to tap her foot. "I know this," she said. "I was the one who showed you the tacky flyer Keith's committee sent asking us to the wine tasting, at only two hundred dollars a pop."

Nate shook his silvery head, chuckling. "I hadn't re-alized they were asking so much."

"You didn't read the fine print. Go on."

"Okay, so there was the election issue, and of course Gabe's total opposition to the building in the quarry—"

"Not for the most altruistic reasons," Wally broke in. "Not for environmental or economic reasons, unless you count what his house's value would be diminished by if the building went forward."

"I thought you liked Gabe."

"I do."

"Then why are you acting like he is some kind of self-centered only-out-for-himself person?"

"I'm just saying, he isn't opposed to the building for the same reason you and I and our environmental friends are, or the board of education-we-can't-afford-to-build-new-schools people are, or the preserve-Grosvenor-and-never-make-a-single-change-slash-improvement types."

"His points are valid, even if he isn't from one of your imagined factions."

"I'll concede that," said Wally, since her mind had suddenly taken off in a new direction. "Why were the police so interested in his yard?"

"The trajectory of Keith's body seems to indicate he fell or was pushed from Gabe's backyard."

"But it's fenced. That's why I never feel terrified when I'm there for one of his and Petra's summer parties. So how could Keith fall?"

"The fence was down. He was having it replaced with a chain-link fence. So were a lot of his neighbors."

"Oh."

Nate nodded. "Right."

"So this couldn't have happened if the whole fence issue hadn't been brought up?"

Nate narrowed his eyes. "You're not thinking that this is because of Kelley Peren, are you?"

"Of course not. That's absurd. She couldn't have had anything to do with Keith, could she?"

"I don't know. Probably not. Why do you have that look on your face?"

"I was just wondering how many people knew about the fence replacement?"

Nate scowled. "I guess all the people who live around there, and maybe their gardeners, not to mention the contractor who seems to have gotten most of the business. Do you think we should add them all to our suspect list?"

His tone having just narrowly missed sarcasm, Wally didn't immediately respond. Would he prefer to believe it was Gabe Ferry rather than expand the search for the murderer?

"You may have a point," Nate conceded without Wally having to utter a word. "Unless it was just convenient that the fences were down, someone may have actually lured Keith up there to kill him."

"It does seem possible."

"I would say farfetched, but I know I'll get another one of those looks."

Wally narrowed her eyes. "What look?"

"Never mind." Wally was about to press him when the phone rang. Nate picked it up.

It was Norman, and from what Wally could gather of the conversation, he was worried about something. "I'll see what we can do," Nate promised, before hanging up the phone.

"What's wrong?" Wally asked.

"Norman wants us to do something about Keith's murder. He's afraid Dolores Hampton will not want to spend her money in a town where murderers live."

"She can't know the murderer lives here."

"It doesn't matter if it's true or not, it's just important what she thinks. And can you imagine how she would feel if she found out that the person submitting the exhibit proposal for the museum, Gabe, is a suspect? I told Norman we would do what we could, at least a little bit."

"I don't really know what we could do, but I'll keep my ears open." Wally thought a moment. "It seems the police know more about the actual murder than we do."

Nate shrugged. "It's only fair, I suppose." Although he looked serious, his lips turned up at the corners.

"Very funny. But we can't do a whole lot if we don't know how they know about where Keith fell and exactly what time they think it happened. I was under the impression it was after dark, but not really late."

"You're thinking night joggers might have seen something, aren't you? But if you're thinking that, no offense, wouldn't you guess the police are too?"

Wally nodded. "Of course. That isn't my point. Doesn't Gabe go running every night?"

"Yes, I think so."

"Then he was probably not home with Petra. I remember that neither of them was at the park. That means Gabe needs an alibi."

Nate furrowed his brow. "I suppose. But getting back to your Keith was lured to the scene of the crime theory, just how would someone lure him to Gabe's backyard?"

"I can only think of one logical person who could have gotten him there. The person who lived there."

"Gabe? But he wouldn't have done that." Nate's eyes took on a worried look. "Come on, you know him. He isn't like that."

Wally agreed. It was time to go find out who might be like that.

"Where are you going?" asked Nate, when Wally rushed out of the kitchen on her way upstairs.

"To the pool."

Nate followed her. "Why?"

"Because people's tongues are probably wagging

and I want to be there to listen. With any luck someone might let something slip."

"Can I come with you?"

"Who's going to talk if you are sitting there?"

"What do you mean?"

"Nate, you're just not one of the girls." She ignored the befuddled look on his face. She had work to do.

Chapter Six

Dominique led the questioning of the bereaved's ex-wife, Merle Hollis, and his twin daughters, Lara and Amber, since Ryan had become totally tongue-tied when he saw the girls ogling him. He should have been used to that, since he was what many girls would think was pretty cute, but it seemed to make him uncomfortable. It was a setback, Dominique thought ruefully. Ryan's progress was so erratic it was a wonder she was able to put up with him.

But she'd never admit defeat. He may not have been the person she would have chosen for a partner, but she was going to stick it out and make him a good detective. She'd been given a big break when she finally made detective and she was more than happy to pass along her good fortune. Besides, it wasn't like there were millions of applicants for the job of detective in the town of Grosvenor. Most of the time it wasn't detective work that they did at all. It was a step on the way to a better job, however, and that's where Dominique was headed. And all those voices telling her to be happy with what she had, to start having babies with James—who was the envy of all her friends—and wasn't she afraid she'd lose him if she kept saying no, would have to be ignored. She would decide for herself. And until she could get that job with the county, where Detectives Davis and Brady worked, she'd stay in Grosvenor, where nothing much happened.

Lately though, or at least for the last few years, there had been several murders to keep the police occupied. And even though the county had the primary responsibility for the cases, Dominique had fought hard to be included and she wasn't about to let her partner's shortcomings interfere in any way. So she conducted the questioning, delicately, remembering that this family, already torn apart by divorce, had lost a member. Hopefully Ryan would learn a few things. At least he was improving.

"I know you've already talked to Detective Davis," she said, wondering if the gruff detective had thought to spare the feelings of the teenagers. She'd rarely seen him have such consideration, though, so she didn't hold out much hope. "But I want you to go over the events of the evening of July fourth with me."

Merle was the first to speak. "I went to the fireworks with some friends. Then I went home. I was there until I got a call saying that Keith's body had been found."

"That wasn't until almost noon," Dominique said. "You didn't go out before then?"

"Just to walk the dog. But I wasn't anywhere near the quarry."

The first Hollis family lived in a small house near the center of town. Ryan's research had shown that they once lived on the hill overlooking Manhattan and the quarry. Perhaps, Dominique thought, that was where Keith Hollis got the idea to build a housing development in it.

"Who was it who called about Keith?"

"My sister. She heard about it from her neighbor, whose son was one of the boys who found the b—"

Lara started to weep. Her mother handed her a tissue and held her tightly.

Amber's face, while identical to Lara's, bore no such grief. She seemed, if anything, angry. Dominique could understand that, she supposed. If someone had killed someone she loved, she'd feel angry, too. Maybe she could use that anger to get something more than the minimal answers she'd heard so far. "Amber," she said, "when was the last time you saw your father?"

The girl's face went chalk white under the tan that Dominique learned Amber had started cultivating when she went to the Jersey shore at the end of school. She and her sister had been part of a group of girls who had rented a house for the week starting immediately after graduation.

Her voice was barely above a whisper. "Before we went down the shore."

"How would you say that meeting went?"

Amber and Lara looked at each other. If there really was a secret language between twins, they were using it. Dominique saw no actual changes in their expressions, but they suddenly seemed to sit up straighter and look at her in exactly the same way.

"The same way as they always do," said Amber. "We met for dinner and we fought about money. He didn't want to give us a check for the week down the shore and he was pleading poverty to cover up the fact that he didn't love us enough to care what we needed."

The look on Ryan's face told Dominique that not only couldn't he keep a poker face, but that he was having a hard time understanding how a person could need to spend a week down the shore in an incredibly overpriced little house that wasn't much more than a shack in most cases. She supposed he and his many siblings had never "needed" to do that and if they had wanted to, they, like she herself, would have found a way to pay for it on their own.

From the looks of the house they now lived in, Dominique would not have thought the girls could be that spoiled. She flipped her notebook back a few pages to see how long the Hollises had been divorced and how long the three of them had lived in this modest way.

Six years. Merle and Keith Hollis had been officially divorced for six years, so these girls had probably lived a fairly extravagant life, if what Ryan had learned was true, until they were at least ten. Long enough to have gotten used to it and have trouble and regret living without it, especially if their father had not only cut his wife off, but been stingy with his daughters.

"What my daughter means to say," said Merle, "is that her father not only paid only the minimal amount he could for their child support, and nothing into their college fund, he didn't give of himself or consider their feelings. Even if he didn't have the money to pay for their vacation, he could have been happy for them. Instead he just told them they were ungrateful bloodsuckers, threw some money on the table, and left the restaurant. It wasn't enough to cover dinner and I had to come over there with my credit card to pay for it."

Amber's look at Dominique held a challenge, as if saying she dared Dominique to find something good in a person like that. In contrast, Lara just looked sad. "We just wanted to have a nice dinner," she said. "We would have paid him back once we started getting paychecks from our summer jobs. He just didn't wait to hear that. I wish he had, then the last things we said to each other wouldn't have been so horrible."

"What did you say?"

"Nothing that bad," said Amber. "Just something about he could drop dead. But everyone says things like that, don't they?"

Dominique could no more imagine saying that to her father than her father calling her a bloodsucker. She felt even more sorry for these girls.

But she wasn't here as their guidance counselor or family therapist, she was here to try to find out what she could to solve the murder of the twins' father. So far she hadn't learned anything useful. "When did you return from the shore?"

"Right before the fireworks. We wouldn't miss them."

"Your father was there. Are you saying you didn't see him?"

"No. I saw one or two of his buddies, but not him."

"Who?"

"Neal Dawson and Graham Fraser," said Merle. "But I don't know if they saw him that night."

"Have Dawson and Fraser been friends with Mr. Hollis for long?"

"Yes," said Merle, seeming irritated, "or else how would I know them?"

"Could we please have their addresses?"

"You'll have to look them up. Are you thinking they had something to do with it?"

"They may have been among the last people to see him alive."

All three Hollises looked shocked. "Neither of them would hurt anyone," said Amber.

"They were always nice to us," Lara added.

Dominique looked at Merle to see if she would confirm her daughters' assessment. She looked at both her children, shrugged and said, "I don't know anything anymore. And I obviously haven't for years."

Wally got to the pool just as the parents of the day campers were leaving to get dinner ingredients before the buses came to drop off their little ones. From experience, Wally knew that they hoped their children were so tired from their busy days of sun and fun that they would zone out while dinner was being prepared. With the long days of sunlight, there was plenty of time for more fun after dinner, when they were refreshed from their rest.

It was too early for working people, at least ones with regular business hours, to arrive for their evening laps. Luckily, there was no swim meet scheduled for that evening, so Wally could spend as much time poolside as she wanted.

She found her friend Louise under a big hat and swaddled in a gauzy cover-up. "I don't understand why you bother to sit in the sun," Wally said, after she had arranged her towel and pool bag to her liking. "You are covered from head to toe."

"I like the sun. I just don't want it to get to my skin." She was quiet while Wally rubbed sun block on herself. "You think that's going to do something?"

"I never burn."

"No, you just get a nice healthy tan. But you'll be sorry. You'll wrinkle like a prune."

"They call them dried plums, nowadays."

Louise threw her hands up in disgust. "Since when?"

"I couldn't say." Wally looked at her suddenly grumpy friend. "Is something wrong?"

"I lost a sale today," Louise admitted.

"What? I thought the housing market was so hot people were having bidding wars just to knock down the houses and build even bigger ones. What happened to your clients?"

"They got scared off by the stories about the building in the quarry and the murder. They didn't want to get into something that was so iffy."

"What's iffy?"

"The house they were looking at was next door to the Ferrys. They were worried about the building in the quarry, worried about the cliff, and worried about their potential next door neighbor being a murderer. And they aren't the only ones."

"People really think Gabe bashed Keith Hollis's head and pushed him over the edge?"

"Who else would have been able to lure Keith up to his yard?"

"Lure? You think Gabe said, 'Hey, Keith, why don't you come up to my backyard so I can bump you off while the fence is down?' I don't think so."

Louise cocked her big hat at Wally. "What if he said, 'Come watch the fireworks. I have a great view.'"

Wally scowled. "They weren't exactly friends."

"Look," said Louise, "I like Indiana Jones just as much as you do, but do you have a better theory?"

"No. But that's why I'm here."

"You're going to investigate the murder here at the pool?"

"Not really, but I am going to find out what I can. Norman asked Nate and me for help. Don't you two talk?"

"We do a lot more than that. And I guess I understand. He's been worried about what would happen to the museum bid if the case doesn't get solved quickly. So what are you planning to do?"

"From what you say, there are a lot of people talking about it. Most of what they say is probably rumor, but somewhere there may be a snippet of truth. I'm hoping to hear it."

"Where should we start?"

"We?"

"Face it, Wally. If you start walking around alone and striking up conversations, everyone is going to know what you're doing. If I go with you, they'll just think we're having fun at the pool."

Wally thought about it and realized she had a point. "Fine, but first I'm going to do some laps. I may as well get my exercise in while I am trying to look like I'm having fun." She pulled off her cover-up and kicked off her sandals.

"That will be very convincing. Have a good time."

"You aren't coming?"

"Heaven forbid. Not before the sun goes down."

"You sound like a vampire."

Louise bared her teeth.

Wally went over to the deep end and dived in, then worked her way over to one of the lap lanes. She counted out twenty-five and was pleased to see they took her less time to do than they had earlier in the week. When she had toweled off, she and Louise grabbed their wallets and went to get some drinks at the snack bar. Then, carefully avoiding the swarms of bees around the trash cans, they found seats in the snack area and opened their ears.

Some of Merle Hollis's fellow teachers were under a wide shade tree talking about the murder. Louise took an obvious look at the sky and motioned Wally under the same tree. "I just can't risk the sunlight," she said somewhat loudly, by way of explanation.

Resisting another vampire remark, Wally followed her. The temporary cessation of the women's conversation lasted only long enough for the two newcomers to be assessed. Then they started talking again, although in somewhat quieter voices.

There were three of them, all with pool bags bulging with magazines, sun block, water bottles, and nibbles. Wally was fairly sure she recognized one of them from synagogue.

"We have the house in Avon from July twentieth until August third," said one of the women. She was wearing a long mumu with a brightly colored flower pattern. "After that much time with my kids in that little bungalow, I'll be looking forward to school starting up again."

"You say the same thing every year about going down the shore and you always come back saying how great it was," said another woman, who was covered by a long T-shirt.

"Not since the oldest one turned sixteen. It's been downhill from there."

"What was that about the hill?" said an older woman whom Wally suddenly realized had taught in the middle school when Rachel was there. Her name was Colleen, if Wally remembered correctly.

"We were talking about going down the shore," said the mumu wearer. "What were you talking about?"

"I heard," said Colleen, "that Merle and Keith had a big argument at the hill that night."

"I didn't know she was there. My husband and I invited her to go with us, but she said she was staying home."

"Oh, that's strange," said the woman in the T-shirt.

Wally thought so too. It might bear looking into.

The conversation turned to food just then. By the time the women left, Wally's stomach was growling.

"I'm going home to toss a salad," said Louise. "Although I suppose that even though it's so hot out, you'll still make a four-course dinner."

Wally nodded, but she conceded, "I made it earlier, when it was cool."

Louise shook her head. "You are too much." She picked up her pool bag. "Coming?"

"No." Wally had just seen Georgia Dewey, a day care provider whose many charges often ended up in one of Wally's classes. She lived right across the street from Ron Walsh's house, where Keith Hollis was staying until he died. "I'll see you later."

After Louise packed up, Wally went over to Georgia's chair. "How are you?" she asked, taking the seat next to her.

"Good. The last child was picked up fifteen minutes ago."

"You didn't waste any time getting over here," Wally said, chuckling.

"It's what I live for in the summer."

They spent a few minutes discussing the four students that were in Wally's nursery class and went to day care after school. "They spend most of their time telling me about you," she told Georgia.

"Funny, they spend a lot of time afterwards telling me about you. It was always, 'Wally said this, and we did this with Wally.'"

"It's scary, sometimes, the impact we have on their lives, isn't it?"

Georgia shrugged. "I guess. They keep me too busy to think about it."

"I know what you mean. You are so busy keeping an eye on them, you probably don't have a chance to see what's going on outside your door."

Georgia's face registered momentary puzzlement before she got a really sly look. "I am never too busy to know what's going on around me. That's why I was so helpful to the police."

Wally tried to cover her surprise with an impressed expression. She had hoped something might come of the conversation but she didn't want to make Georgia clam up. "When did you talk to them?"

"Right after the murder. I think they were talking to everyone on my block. I told them all about the gay brothel."

She said that as if it was nothing unusual. Wally tried to cover her own reaction to that statement and waited for an explanation.

"All hours of the day and night those men go in and out. At first I thought that Ronny was running a drug trade, but then when I saw the men carrying in suitcases I realized what it was. Although I don't know why they would have stayed all night and gotten their mail delivered there." She shook her head, obviously puzzled.

Wally had wondered why Keith Hollis lived where he did after his separation but she felt reasonably sure that Georgia's conclusions were wrong. She made a note to ask Dominique what the story was since it wasn't likely she'd get the real truth from Georgia. But if she could get some information, it was worth continuing the conversation. "Did you ever talk to Keith?"

A cloud passed over Georgia's expression. "Yes. And while I don't ordinarily speak ill of the dead, I'll say this. Whoever killed him did the world a big favor."

"He made a lot of people unhappy," Wally said, by way of agreement. She was nearly bursting, hoping to find out what Georgia knew. Whatever it was sounded mighty close to home for the caregiver.

"He had a lot of nerve."

"Really?"

"I mean, can you imagine him butting into my business like that? Like he had a clue or a right to express it."

Wally shook her head and tsked tsked. "You're not saying he criticized you? The queen of day care providers?" She hoped she hadn't laid that on too thick.

Georgia beamed, but then frowned. "Not in his mind."

"What happened?" Wally asked, unwilling to continue the verbal volleyball and hoping to get to the point.

"He was looking for a package. He said he saw the Federal Express truck stop in front of the house but couldn't get to the door in time and he thought the guy delivered it to me to give to him. This was half an hour later. What was he doing that he couldn't get to the door, I ask you? And what took him a half hour to come look for the package?"

Wally shrugged.

"And what am I," Georgia added, "some sort of delivery service?" She took a sip from her water bottle and fixed Wally with a look that said she most certainly was not.

"Of course not," Wally said, leaning forward. She hoped her body language would move this story along.

"So I told him I couldn't look for it right then because one of the children was crying." She paused.

"You have your priorities," Wally agreed. "Go on."

"And he said he'd seen me through the window, sleeping on the couch, not watching the children, and that if I didn't get the package right away, he'd tell the parents of the children that my house was dangerous and that I was neglectful. I wasn't sleeping, I told him, the children and I were playing hide and seek and I was counting to twenty. It wasn't his business anyway. Then I stuffed that stupid package into his hand and closed the door in his face."

"Did you ever meet those other people who lived there?"

"Meet them? No. But I saw a lot of them, always moving cars around, arguing with Keith or barbequing on Ronny's grill. That man is too nice. But maybe he's just trying to take care of people like him."

Wally concluded they were back to the gay brothel theory and steered clear. "Did you see anyone else?"

"Haven't you been listening? Lots of people. Some came when only Keith was home. I think he had a poker night there on Wednesdays, because I could smell cigar smoke when I walked my dog in front of the house."

"Was that when you heard arguing?"

"No, there was a lot of drunken laughter, though.

And I could hear their bets. We weren't talking about penny ante stuff, either."

"When did the arguments happen?"

"Keith came storming out of the house one day, shouting at someone inside. Then he got in his car and drove off, way over the speed limit. A few minutes later that Norville Morgan came out, and he got into his car and drove off, although he wasn't speeding."

"When was that?"

"Back in May."

"Do you think they were fighting about a poker game?"

"Nope. It wasn't a Wednesday and besides, that man doesn't play with Keith."

Wally admired Georgia's recollections and observations. "What about Ronny? Do you think he liked having Keith there?"

"He's such a nice guy he probably wouldn't have said anything even if he didn't. But he's also away a lot. He says he stays at his girlfriend's house, but we both know that couldn't be true."

Wally briefly wondered why not, but remembered Georgia's ridiculous theory. It didn't seem to fit with poker-playing cigar-smoking, beer-swilling, big-bet-making men, but what did she know? "Have you told all this to the police?"

"They didn't ask me. But I'm sure none of it is important."

Wally wasn't so sure, and she made another mental note to talk to Dominique about it as soon as she was free.

* * *

When Wally got home the light on her answering machine was blinking and indicated there were seven messages. They all turned out to be about the same thing but Wally had to listen to all of them to piece together the information. Abby had fallen over something in the restricted construction area of the nursery school when she went to check on the installation and she had broken her leg. She was expected to recover completely but in the meantime Wally would have to act as administrator as well as teach her class. And she was now in charge of the construction.

Chapter Seven

Wally called Dominique early in the day, before the day camp started. They sorted out the real reason why those men were staying at Ron Walsh's house and Wally told Dominique the other information she'd learned from Georgia about the arguments and the Wednesday night poker games.

"Do you think maybe one of the poker players was angry enough at Keith to kill him?" Wally suggested.

"We'll track them down and see what they have to say," Dominique promised. "Morgan, too. I can also tell you that we're trying to talk to Keith's two friends who may have been with him at some point on the night of the murder." Dominique lowered her voice. "Captain Jaeger is making a lot of noise about how long this is taking."

"It's been hardly any time at all. Five, six days, tops."

"He's feeling pressure from the county, who says without Elliot's help we couldn't solve a bicycle theft."

"That isn't true."

"What can I say? We're kind of short on leads and long on suspects. Every time I talk to someone else, more possibilities come up. Like your conversation with Mrs. Dewey. She had a lot more to say to you."

"I basically just listen. People tend to talk to me. I sometimes think they are trying to fill the void of silence I create by not taking over the conversation."

Dominique laughed. "Good technique. I'm not sure it would work for me, but it seems to work for you."

"Then you don't mind if I keep asking questions? Norman Fisch is worried about what Dolores Hampton might think if we have an unsolved murder of a developer in town. She might think the people of Grosvenor don't take kindly to improvements, such as her museum, and decide to give the money and everything else to another town."

"Go right ahead and ask around," said Dominique. "As long as you don't let people think it's official. Oh, and there's one more thing. It hasn't been publicized yet but I thought you'd like to know. We've matched a shovel to one of the wounds in Keith Hollis's skull."

"Whose fingerprints were on the shovel?"

"Only those of the workers at the site. No others were found."

"Someone thought to wear gloves?"

"Probably not. We think maybe the shovel was wiped off. There is a micro fiber stuck to a splinter on the shovel. It seems to be from some kind of jacket material. But it's quite common. We're looking anyway."

"I hope you find it. It would end this nightmare."

"I wish," said Dominique. "Good luck with your questions."

As Wally hung up she knew all of that would have to wait until later. For now she had to get ready to be on the school's receiving line. Abby had finally settled on one door for bringing the children into the building and if it weren't for her insisting on bringing them out a different door, most of the confusion would have been over. Even though she was now in charge, Wally opted to keep the system, crazy as it was, for the present, since at least everyone knew what to expect.

Before she could get her own class settled, she was called to the office by one of the parents who had volunteered to help in the crisis. "I'll watch your class," the mom said, "I know what to sing. Danny sings it all afternoon every day when he gets home."

Wally had no time to worry that she was getting predictable and stale before she saw the man wearing a tool belt, work clothes, and a frown. Wally explained who she was and why she was there. "Are you the gentleman I spoke to on the phone about the computer wiring?"

"Yes," said the man. "I'm Van Shepherd. The general contractor. The guy who is about to walk off this job and take his chances with the lawsuits if I ever have to deal with that woman again. I don't care if she sues me for what happened yesterday. It isn't our fault. That ladder was not there for her use."

The reason for her being there had been the focus of one of the phone calls Wally received about Abby. She was supposedly trying to check the quality of the new partitioning by getting on a ladder and looking around. The ladder had not been properly secured before she got up on it. There was no question that the whole thing was Abby's fault.

But this man did not seem to be worrying about a lawsuit, at least not against his company. He was angry about Abby's micromanaging what was not her job—the construction. "Tell me what's wrong," Wally said, hoping she didn't sound as if she were talking to a five-year-old, even if that's how the two supposed adults were acting.

Van narrowly missed whining. "She keeps telling me what to do. It's not like everything we're doing here isn't in the blueprints we gave the board."

"I'm sure she understands that. But in Abby's defense, she wasn't consulted at all. Maybe there is something that wouldn't really work in the classrooms and she's right. And maybe it's something that wouldn't be too hard to fix."

Van narrowed his eyes. "We'll see. Come this way."

He took her over to what looked like a roughed out bathroom and pointed at the frame. "This is what she's screaming about. She wants us to hang the door on the other side, but then it would interfere with the door to the hallway."

Wally saw the problem immediately. "If you hang it the way you want, we won't be able to see in from the classroom."

"Why do you need to see in?"

"These are young children. We need to know if there are problems. They usually leave the door open at least a little bit."

"Hmm." Van pondered the problem while Wally did the same. She saw no solution but he managed to come up with one that would work. It involved an expensive change in the door construction, but it was a good remedy. "Someone should have mentioned this when we did the plans," Van said.

"You're right. It would have saved everyone a lot of trouble and money."

"You are much easier to deal with than your director. Can you be in charge from now on?"

Wally would rather do almost anything but that. It would cut into all that free time she saw herself having this summer to spend with her grandchildren, once the murder was solved, and was sure to be a major headache. She had already been told there was not a good alternative. It seemed, however, that Van didn't know the extent of Abby's injuries and that she was totally out of commission. "Sure," said Wally. "It's not like I have a choice."

It was broiling hot in the kitchen, even with the air conditioner on, and Wally sweated over the Buffalo wings she was bringing to the barbeque. She'd also made a carrot cake with little marzipan carrots complete with pistachio nut stems decorating the cream cheese frosting. She was running a bit late because she had stopped off to check on Debbie's and Elliot's house on the way home. They'd only been gone for a week but so much had happened since they left. It was so unreal. At least the house was okay and their house plants hadn't keeled over from the heat.

"Pot luck?" Nate asked, when he came into the kitchen. "Cameron Buxton asked us to bring food?"

"I offered," Wally confessed. "When Cyd called, she sounded a bit overwhelmed. It seems a lot more people accepted her invitation than she'd thought, and she wanted more ideas for variety. I suggested the wings and cake, and she thanked me so much for offering."

"Typical of her," Nate noted. "You fall for it every time."

Wally took the last batch of wings out of the oven. "What's the big deal? I do this for Louise all the time."

"That's different." He shrugged and took several heads of celery out of the refrigerator. "I may as well help out."

"Good idea. And don't forget to leave some wings for Mark. He'd never forgive me if there weren't any for him to snack on."

While they worked, Wally filled Nate in on her conversation with Dominique. "What would make a person angry enough to bash someone in the head and throw him over a cliff?" she wondered aloud.

Nate had no answer for her.

The Buxtons lived on the hill, the ritziest part of Grosvenor, right next to the Frieds, who were still on their trip to Africa. Their house seemed dark and lifeless compared to the festivities going on next door.

The Buxtons' manicured, meticulously landscaped

backyard opened onto the bottom part of the quarry, and seemed endless, even though it was bordered on all sides by a high, green-clad, chain-link fence to keep their Labradoodle and their Japanese Chin in and the deer out. Just beyond the fence the wilds of the over-grown quarry spread out for acres. There was an incline which looked as if it could have once been a road, that circled around to the top, making the quarry depth un-even. Some houses that backed onto that old road had small drops from their backyards. As the road wound up and finally petered out, the drops increased; the houses on the top were on sheer cliffs that plunged to the bottom of the quarry pit. Gabe Ferry's was one of those houses. Wally shivered at the thought.

Tall tiki torches in attractive planters dotted the fence perimeter in an effort to discourage mosquitoes. Ever since West Nile virus had come to New Jersey people were paying a lot more attention to the unwanted wildlife. That included the tick-carrying deer. Wally detected the scent of anti-flea-and-tick spray mingling with the smell of citronella candles and was glad that she had insisted that she and Nate wear repellant.

Wally set down the platter of Buffalo chicken wings, celery, and blue cheese dressing for those purists who insisted that the wings be served the way they had orig-inally been served in the Anchor Bar in Buffalo, New York. Seconds later, the platter was empty, devoid of everything but the bones, celery, and blue cheese dress-ing. Nate gave Wally an "I told you no one needs those other things" look and winked.

"Hmph," she said.

"What?" asked Louise, who was wearing a long, yellow sun dress and large straw hat which was a little too big and way too floppy. Wally smoothed her off white linen slacks and sat down next to her friend.

"Nothing. Nate was having a smug moment. I was giving my opinion of its merit."

"Oh. What have you found out about the murder?"

"Nothing much."

"Well, here's your chance to talk to Merle Hollis."

Wally looked around and after a few seconds, spotted Merle talking to Cyd Buxton. "It's nice to see she's getting out."

Louise nodded. "Are you going to question her?"

"What are you talking about?" Wally asked, trying to sound innocent.

Her friend knew her too well and said so. "Did Dominique ask you for help?"

"No, of course not. She's an excellent detective and she can solve this case with one hand tied behind her back and both eyes closed."

"Not to mention, in her sleep."

Wally stared at Louise. "Have you been drinking?"

Louise shook her head. "How long is it going to take for you to make your way over to Merle and start pumping her for answers? There's a lot at stake here, and I don't just mean Keith's murder."

"I've already expressed my condolences and asked how she was doing only two days ago when I saw her at the bank. Wouldn't it seem awfully obvious if I went over and started to pump her?"

"Yes, it would. So I am going there with you."

"Okay. But stay behind me."

"As if I could hide behind you."

"And take off your hat. The sun is behind those trees anyway."

Louise complied. "Fine, but I'm warning you, the woman is a shrew."

While Wally had seen Merle be sharp with people, she was sure that was only an aberration. "I didn't know you knew her."

"I don't exactly. But I told you what I heard when I was selling her neighbors' house and got the scoop on Merle and Keith's divorce. It appears that Merle can cut your heart out with her tongue."

Wally started to open her mouth but Louise held up her hand. "But I know you've known her for years and your mind is made up. And I promise when it comes time for you two to be alone, I will be at the buffet table filling my plate."

Together they worked their way around the huge crowd toward their goal: Merle.

She was sitting alone by that point, although there were several people nearby, many of whom were speaking in hushed tones as if talking about the poor woman. Wally brushed past them and took a seat on Merle's left side. Louise took one on the right.

"How are you doing?" Wally asked.

Merle gave Wally a weak smile. "Lara and Amber liked the food you brought for dinner that night," she said. "I should have thanked you."

The twins had been in Wally's class for a school year and two summers, which made them practically family

in times of need. "It was the least I could do," Wally
said honestly. "I wish I could be of more help."

Now that she was seeing her under more normal circumstances, Wally realized that Merle had changed a
lot from when the twins were in nursery school. She was
still quite a petite woman but she'd lost some of the ani-
mation in her face. Even her hair hung limply, though
that could have been attributable to the heat. Wally, who
had showered five minutes before getting into the car to
come to the barbeque, already felt sticky herself.

"I feel so sorry for the girls," Wally said. "How are
they doing?"

"As well as can be expected. I think their grief is all
mixed up with guilt and it isn't helping."

"Guilt?"

"They had a fight with their father and had not recon-
ciled before he was killed."

"How sad."

"I'm going to get them some counseling. They'll be
okay."

"I'd like you to meet my friend, Louise Fisch,"
Wally said.

Merle smiled at her, and Wally could see her losing
some of her tension.

"If you'll excuse me," Louise said, after exchanging
pleasantries, "I'm starving. Can I get either of you
anything?"

"No, thanks," said Wally. Merle declined also.
Louise left the two of them alone.

"I get the sense that people are talking about me,"
Merle said, watching Louise walk over to the buffet table.

"Louise isn't like that," Wally said, although she knew it wasn't a hundred percent true. Louise had a tendency to repeat things she had heard without checking on how true they were. Then again, she had passed along useful information on occasion.

"I didn't mean Louise. I know she's a friend of yours."

Wally was more interested in what she had overheard Colleen say about Merle arguing with Keith on the evening of his murder. But there didn't seem to be a way to get right down to it. She looked out past the fence into the darkening quarry.

Merle followed her gaze and shivered. "I guess I shouldn't have come here. I didn't realize it was right on the quarry."

"I'm sorry," said Wally. "It must be so hard for you."

"I think what's harder is not knowing who . . ."

"You can't think it's someone you know, do you?"

Merle looked at Wally with pain in her eyes. "It's unlikely to be someone I don't know. Unless it was someone Keith had dealings with out of town. But then how would the person know about where—"

Wally filled in the rest of that sentence in her mind. Merle meant where to hit Keith and push him off in order to kill him.

"No one in town would have felt so strongly about the proposals for the quarry to do that," said Wally, with confidence she didn't quite feel. It was quite possible she was wrong and she'd recently found herself looking at her neighbors in a new light. She knew she would mentally apologize to everyone she wondered about once the murderer was found, but she wanted the awful feelings of distrust to stop. It was all the more reason for her to do her bit to solve the case. She hated feeling suspicious of her neighbors.

Merle shook her head. "There were a lot of people angry at Keith and not just for the quarry. I hated him myself. Without me he'd be nothing. And after all I did for him and the way he dumped me, he griped about every cent of alimony he had to pay me. I had a fight with him that night," she said, before covering her mouth. Her voice had been rising and becoming more angry sounding with every word. She took a deep breath, and said, barely above a whisper, "I was so mad at how he treated the girls. I didn't kill him, though."

"Of course not," said Wally, deciding to accept this as the truth, at least for the time being. "But who hated him that much?"

"Anyone who didn't fall for that charming act of his. Or maybe even someone who did, but who suddenly got a glimpse of the real Keith. He could turn into such a monster and just as quickly back to Mr. Charm and Personality, once he got what he wanted."

Wally remembered how Keith could sweet talk people. He'd made an appearance at the senior citizen building where Tillie, Nate's mother, lived. After one afternoon with him, half the women in the building were convinced they'd found a new boyfriend. With his handsome face and tons of appeal, anyone who didn't know him well would think he practically walked on water.

Merle wasn't finished. "He was mean and vindictive and sneaky and manipulative. He treated Tori nearly as badly as he treated me, and he was even nasty to his friends. I think they were ready to write him off."

"Who?"

"Neal and Graham, for sure."

"Has he known them long?"

"They were in high school together. He had already lost his other friends, the ones on the football team. I never saw that coming. They used to do everything together. They were the talk of the high school. Then one day they all split up."

Wally sensed that learning some things about Keith's background might be useful. "What were they like in high school?"

"Oh, they got into their share of scrapes. Two of them weren't exactly star students either. If I hadn't tutored Keith he would have flunked. But they were good at football and a lot of shortcomings were overlooked."

"Did they ever get into trouble with the police?"

"Funny you should ask. In trouble? Not exactly. In fact, they probably believed they were helping the police."

"In what way?"

"I don't know if you remember, but about twenty-five years ago, when Keith and I were in high school, there were some problems in Circle Park."

Circle Park was the one closest to the edge of town, near Newark. It had seen it's share of trouble over the years, but lately had been lauded as an example of what a good city park should be. "I remember," Wally said.

"There were gangs of kids coming in from Newark, mugging people and using the proceeds to buy and sell drugs. Keith and his buddies got the cops to look the other way while they "cleaned up" the park.

"Do you mean they beat up those kids?"

"It isn't like they were innocent children," Merle pointed out. "But yes. At least until Keith gave his kidney to his sister. Not much happened after that, maybe one or two incidents, and Keith couldn't have been part of it. At least not physically."

"What about his other friends, Graham Fraser and Neal Dawson?"

"Oh, his poker buddies. They're also old friends, although from after the time Keith left the football team. He started a band with them." She stopped, as if remembering. "I don't really know Neal all that well, since I haven't talked to him in years, but Graham is nice. He's really torn up over Keith's death."

"I take it you've talked to him?"

"We've been seeing each other."

"Did Keith know?"

"I don't know. It wasn't his business, anyway." Merle stared at Wally, open mouthed. "Unless . . . you don't think Graham could have anything to do with it . . . ?"

Wally didn't know what to think. But what she thought didn't matter, until it was what she knew, and she was no closer to knowing anything than before. "Did you see Neal and Graham at the fireworks?"

"Neal? No? Graham and I were together that night, though." She smiled slightly.

"Do you think Keith saw you with him?"

"No, I met Graham there later, after I talked to Keith."

"So you saw the fireworks together?"

"Actually, no. There were so many people there we couldn't find one another until they were over." Merle cocked her head to one side. "How did you know Graham and Neal's full names?"

Wally realized her mistake and that she had to come clean. "I don't know if you know this, but I have a connection at the police department. Dominique Scott is a friend of mine."

"Does she just go around talking about cases to everyone?"

"No, of course not. It's just that I have helped the police in the past."

She stood up. "Then I hope you believe that I had nothing to do with Keith's death. And that you'll leave me alone. I don't want to talk about it anymore." Without another word, she was gone.

Wally was left with even more vague suspicions and many more questions.

Chapter Eight

Rachel called at 7:30 in the morning. "Adam was called out of town. Again. How would you feel about two and three quarters visitors?"

Wally didn't have to think for a second. "Bring bathing suits."

There was a short silence on the line. "Are you sure Grosvenor is ready for Baby Beluga?"

"You don't look that big, and besides, it's a beautiful thing. Plus, Jody loves the pool."

This time the silence was longer. Wally knew that Rachel and Adam had decided not to join their town pool this summer because the baby was due in early August and their chances of getting there afterwards were slim. The membership was expensive and the cost was a good reason not to join and waste money, which was tight this year, even though Adam was working nearly around the clock. Yet it was a shame for Jody.

She had absolutely loved going last summer and talked about it all winter.

But Wally didn't want to appear to be passing judgment. "It'll be fun," she added, hoping that would be enough.

Rachel, who had always been the less flappable of Wally's two daughters, even when pregnant, laughed. "I should have thought of this sooner."

The tense moment over, Wally needed to plan. "How long will you be staying?"

"How much ice cream do you have?"

Rachel's sweet tooth was still firmly rooted, Wally noticed. "I'll go to the store on my way home from the nursery school. See you when I get home. Unless you'd rather Dad pick you up?"

"I can still get behind the wheel," Rachel assured her. "See you in a few hours."

Wally called Nate and told him the good news. She knew he'd also be happy for the extra time with his daughter and granddaughter. He and Wally had hidden their disappointment when Adam and Rachel bought a house in Westchester instead of New Jersey, but it had made sense for the young couple and she and Nate knew enough to keep quiet. It just meant they saw less of them.

But not this week. Wally brushed off any questions the contractor, Van, had at the nursery school and left as soon as the last child got strapped into the last SUV. Then she ran to the store and stocked up on nutritious food for the gestating baby and fun food for the rest of them. She firmly believed in all five of the food groups, including chocolate.

Jody practically jumped out of the car when Rachel pulled into the driveway. She grabbed her little pink overnight bag and ran to Wally. The four-year-old girl's red pigtails shone in the sunshine and the hug she gave Wally nearly knocked her over.

"Go change into your bathing suit," Wally said. "We have time to go to the pool this afternoon."

"Can we have lunch there?"

"It's already packed up."

Jody was changed in seconds. Rachel took substantially longer. Her face looked flushed from the effort of bringing her things into the house and she was busy pulling her dark hair into a ponytail to help relieve the heat. Wally took note that the baby still hadn't dropped, even though on Rachel's small frame it looked as if she was ready to go any minute.

By one-thirty they were finished with lunch and ensconced in their seats by the wading pool. Wally sat on the side of the pool with her feet in the water while Jody played and Rachel lay on a lounge chair napping. The pool was shaded by the large trees overhead and was cool and peaceful even at that hour.

There was a girl walking over to the pool whose mother looked familiar. When she took off her cover-up, the gold lamé suit underneath jogged Wally's memory and she almost said, "Eureka." Here was her chance to talk to Tori Hollis, Keith's second wife, and she hadn't even needed to seek her out.

Remembering her problem with Merle, Wally chose to be a lot more open about her involvement in the investigation. While she didn't think Captain Jaeger of the police department would vouch for her, even after all the help she'd given him in the past, she did think she was on somewhat solid ground saying she was lending a hand.

As soon as Tori put a washcloth down on the side of the pool to sit on so she wouldn't damage her suit, Wally introduced herself. She whispered her condolences so that the child couldn't hear her. Tori dipped her head in acknowledgement. When she didn't pick it up, Wally realized the woman was crying.

"I'm so sorry," Wally said. "I thought you and Keith were divorcing. But it seems as if you still have feelings for him."

Tori stood up and fished around in her pool bag for her sunglasses, then put them on. For a moment Wally thought she looked familiar, not just from having seen her at the funeral, but the feeling passed. "In more ways than I'd care to admit," Tori said. "But we couldn't be together."

Wally mulled that over while Tori put out a pail and some other water toys for her daughter and set them on the water, but the preschooler stayed close to Tori's leg. Jody looked over at the child and moved toward her in her typical friendly way. "This is my granddaughter, Jody," Wally said. Tori introduced her daughter, Gracie, and soon the two were splashing and playing.

It seemed that the consensus that the marriage wasn't one for love was at least half wrong. That little tidbit would wipe the smug smiles off some people's faces, if Wally could ever mention it to them. Which she couldn't. If she was going to claim to be helping the police then she had to maintain the same confidentiality they did. Or at least something like it.

"I'm really sorry. It must have been so hard."

"It was about to get harder," Tori said, her tone getting harder as well. "In another week, we'd have been out of the house, and I still hadn't found any place for us to go." She gazed at her child again. To Wally, Gracie seemed to be doing a lot better than her mother, but then again, she was probably too small at four to really know that Daddy was never coming back. For all Wally knew, even if Gracie had been told that he was dead, it was really no different than when he'd moved out of the house, and she thought it was just a longer gap between visits.

Wally was still processing what Tori had said about the house. She knew that Keith had sold it, but hadn't realized the deal was not closed. She didn't know whether the death of one party invalidated the whole sale. Louise, since she was a real estate agent, would know, and Wally planned to ask her. Hypothetically, of course, to preserve confidentiality.

"So you are staying in the house?"

"Yes. At least for now. I think any more changes would really hurt Gracie. She's been through enough."

"So have you," Wally said, unable to keep from sympathizing. She knew she was talking to a suspect, at this point practically everyone was under suspicion, but she couldn't help feeling sorry for the woman. Tori had gotten so much less than she'd bargained for when she married Keith.

Jody came over to the side of the pool and pulled Wally's hand for her to come to the center. There the water was only knee deep, or calf deep on most other adults, and Wally held Jody by the waist and let her pretend to swim. Tori's daughter tugged on her hand and she too, came to the center.

"They barely let me be alone with my daughter," Tori said, half to herself.

Wally had to think for a second to realize she was still talking about her ordeal. "Do you mean the police?"

Tori nodded. "I had to talk to them for hours right after they found Keith. I should have been with Gracie."

Wally hadn't been briefed on that conversation yet, because Dominique, when she suggested that Wally should seek Tori out, didn't want her to have any preconceptions. "I guess you would have," she said, noncommittally.

"And I told them I had gone to the fireworks with Gracie and my parents. They were here that whole weekend because we were trying to figure out what to do."

"What had you decided?"

"Nothing definite. Except that I was going to find a job. I didn't want to be dependent on Keith for anything. He would only hold it over my head."

Her hardness was moving into bitterness now. Wally wondered if it was enough to have induced her to kill her ex-husband. The uncertainty about the time of death could have made the timing of those fireworks critical or not important at all. It would have taken people who attended the display, which was nearly everyone who was in town for the holiday, several minutes to get back to their homes, especially the people on top of the hill. No one would have been around to witness anything.

"My daughter told me that Jody loved fireworks but that some of the other children they knew were frightened. How was Gracie?"

Even with her sunglasses on, Wally could tell that Tori's expression changed. "I wasn't with her for that. She stayed with my parents and I took a walk. I just couldn't sit still. But I didn't kill him."

She did have unaccounted time, though. Unless she'd run into someone while she was walking, she didn't have an alibi.

Gracie got out of the pool, went over to one of the chairs and sat down next to it. There was a pool bag beside her, brimming with toys, and she busily removed them. Jody watched for a moment and then pulled Wally out to follow Gracie. Rachel, who was finished with her nap, laughed at her daughter and followed too, just as Tori got to the chair.

Wally was glad for the interruption. She needed to process what she'd just learned and not blow it. "I'd like you to meet someone," she said to Tori and Rachel, introducing the two women, "I'm going to go do some laps."

Jody and Rachel went upstairs to take a late afternoon nap. Wally, freshly showered, was in the kitchen with her fiesta salad ingredients and her thoughts, and she still heard Rachel's words in the car ringing in her ears.

She had been incredulous. "I can't believe you,

Mom. Are you telling me that the whole time you were talking to her you didn't realize that she was Victoria Ford? She certainly knew who you were."

It was acutely embarrassing, and left Wally wondering if she had been having a really long senior moment. How could she not remember one of the girls that Rachel was so close with in middle school? Tori, then known as Vicki, had even attended Rachel's bat mitzvah.

Now that it was all coming back to her, Wally recalled that Vicki had come in dressed as if for a black tie affair. Since the party was right after services, she had looked fancier than either Rachel or Debbie. It hadn't bothered her a bit to be so overdressed.

"I thought she looked familiar for a minute. I guess I should have gone with that."

"She certainly recognized you. That's why she was spilling her guts." Rachel narrowed her eyes. "Or do you really think you are so good at interrogation that complete strangers will open up to you?"

Wally bit her lip. Then she tried to think of a witty retort. The best she could manage was, "She looks very different now."

Rachel smiled, thawing out a bit. "She had her nose done in high school but I didn't know about that, since she went to a private school. And then, since she wanted to be an actress, she had breast implants."

"During college?"

"She ended up not finishing college. She changed her nickname, went off to California, and tried to get into movies."

"But she ended up back here."

Rachel nodded. "From what I could understand, Vicki's, I mean Tori's father brought her back home when she'd hit rock bottom. Then one of his friends introduced Tori to Keith and he pursued her as if she were a princess. Since she was used to being treated that way by her father and had missed it while she was in L.A., she accepted his proposal."

Wally was impressed. Rachel's ability to gather information was even better than her own. But she wouldn't say that, since Rachel was technically talking to a friend and not simply prying.

"Did she tell you that she was about to lose her house, and that she still had feelings about him even though they were divorcing? Didn't that make you wonder about the murder?"

"No, that's your modus operandi, Mrs. Fletcher. But this isn't Cabot Cove. Tori and I talked about hopes and dreams for the future, and other stuff. She's really a warm and sincere woman. She invited Jody and me to lunch on Wednesday."

"That's nice of her."

"Unless you had other plans?" Rachel asked, seeming to suddenly be afraid she was being rude.

How far things have come, thought Wally, from those teenage years. "No problem. I hope you have fun."

Wally paid dearly for her brusque treatment of the contractor working on the nursery school when he summoned her as soon as school started the next day. "I can't get this job done by Labor Day," said Van. "It'll be late October at least."

Doing rapid calculations in her mind, Wally realized that not only would it affect the nursery school and Hebrew school programs, it would also cause problems with the upcoming High Holidays marking the Jewish New Year. The parking lot would still be full of construction vehicles, the building itself would be anything but clean, and the dumpster was in the area where the Sukkah was to be erected, as it was every year after Yom Kippur.

"What's the problem, Van?" Wally asked. "Why will you take so much longer than you promised?"

"Don't get huffy with me," he said. "It isn't like I suddenly realized I made a mistake with my estimates."

"Then what is it?"

"Your town inspectors have been consistently late showing up. Or they cancel and say they'll come their next scheduled day. We can't do anything until we get the work we've already done inspected, so my guys are stuck just sitting around. I can't afford that, so I send them home and they get booked onto other jobs. They can't stop something in the middle, and we fall further behind here. It isn't my fault."

"Inspectors often take a long time to come," Wally said, remembering her own renovations. "Didn't you add that into your calculations?"

Van gave Wally a look that said she must be crazy just about the same time as the little voice in her head said don't make matters worse, try for a solution. She was about to try to cool things down when the contractor said, "I'm not used to this. Most people I work for manage to get the inspectors to the job when they need them."

"How? What can I do to get them here? I'll do it, I promise."

"I sort of doubt it, lady. You don't look like the type to bribe people."

Wally wasn't sure whether that was a compliment or not. "That doesn't seem right," she told him, voicing her opinion of the practice.

"Lotsa people do it. Probably people you know. It's the easiest way."

Wally let that pass. "I don't believe for a minute that the only way to get the inspectors to a job on time is to bribe them. How far in advance do you request them?"

A little squirm, reminiscent of one of Wally's student's attempts to avoid taking responsibility for something, told her that Van was not always making his appointments in a timely manner. "How about if you tell me when you'll need an inspection and I'll make the appointments?" she suggested.

"Go for it," Van said glumly.

She ignored his naysayer attitude. "Okay, I'll do that. But you have to let me know in enough time to arrange it."

Van's arguments seemed to have run their course. He gave one half-hearted final protest. "This is a very unpredictable business."

Too bad Wally didn't have time to soothe him now. "We have to get this job done before school starts in September," she said. "I will do whatever I can, but you can't let us down. Too many people are depending on it to let little things stand in the way." Feeling she'd been firm enough, she added, "I've heard about you from friends and they all say you're the best, that your work is impeccable." She named a few of the people who had told her that and Van smiled appreciatively. "I know you'll make this renovation a big success."

She didn't think it was all in her imagination that Van puffed up a bit and set off to the construction site with new determination.

"We still haven't found out how Hollis got to the top of the hill," Dominique said, sitting down at her desk for the first time all day. "And you know that is going to be the first question Captain Jaeger asks."

"We have asked everyone who admits to seeing him at the fireworks that night," Ryan said. "And we can account for almost every minute of his last twenty-four hours up to the time he left the park," he added, as if he thought Dominique didn't believe him.

She did, of course, because she'd been involved with at least half of the questioning, and knew that Ryan, who had been involved in the other half, since he was partnered with Detective Brady of the prosecutor's office, had covered all his bases. That had been the same pattern for every big investigation in Grosvenor—the county grudgingly let the local police get involved, but only in tandem with the county detectives. Dominique, along with her county prosecutor's office partner, Davis, a jittery, cocksure, impatient man, always went by the book. Even beyond the book, in at least one case, garnering a rare look of appreciation from her partner.

That moment had occurred just as the two of them

were talking to the last of Hollis's golf buddies. The four men had gone out golfing together every Wednesday, weather permitting, and even not permitting in most people's minds, from what Dominique could gather. Keith's three partners were all medical doctors of some kind.

"Were you also doing business together?" Dominique asked J. J. Ogden, the last of the three. He was of medium height and, after he took off his white coat and hung it up, they could see that he was muscular, looking as if he worked out several times a week.

Ogden flexed his biceps, which were barely covered by his pastel polo shirt. Although she suspected the movement was unconscious, Dominique felt a wave of distaste. She liked her man on the athletic side, but preferred that he got his muscles from playing games. James, her husband, played plenty of basketball, football and softball, whatever was in season. Ogden, however, seemed more like the gym type, intentionally working on his body's definition. A quick glance at Davis, to see if he caught the movement, showed he had and was totally disgusted. Then again, to Dominique, he always looked that way.

Ogden wrote something on the chart on his desk, as if he'd just thought of it. There were stacks of charts in the out box on the huge desk, which was decorated with all kinds of golf knickknacks and trophies. There was a picture of the doctor at a black-tie dinner that showed him being honored as a man of the year for his work in getting defibrillators into rescue squad cars, schools, and recreation centers. Dominique remembered hearing about his work when the police department received their defibrillators.

The walls were covered with diplomas indicating that Dr. Ogden was, among other things, board certified in the practice of gastroenterology. Maybe he could do something for the Maalox-popping Davis, Dominique thought.

When he was finished, Dr. Ogden looked up and smiled. "We did some. When Keith had an investment opportunity for us, we took advantage of it. He's made us some money over the years. I don't know what will happen with the current venture, now that he's gone." He frowned. "Such a horrible thing."

"You've known him a long time? Did you go to high school together?"

"Yes, although we lost touch for a few years. My wife and I met him and Merle again soon after we moved to town. Our children were in a play group together. Even after our marriages broke up and our kids got to high school and decided they didn't like each other, we stayed in touch."

"So you were friends?"

A puzzled expression met her question. "He was a friend. We didn't see much of each other, except for our weekly round of golf, though."

That was essentially the same response they'd received from both the other doctors, Fuller and Armour. They weren't close friends who would know any more than about each other's marital status and children. Personal information wasn't shared.

"Dr. Ogden," said Dominique, "we understand you saw Mr. Hollis in the park that evening at about seven-thirty. That was well before the fireworks. Why were you there so early?"

"He knew there were going to be people protesting and wanted to make sure he got a chance to voice his own opinion. Since our money was tied up in the project, he wanted to bring us along."

"But of the three of you, you were the only one who went. Why was that?"

"Fuller is a member of the country club. He said he'd come over after dinner but I guess he couldn't make it."

Since the country club was only about two blocks from the park, Dominique suspected Fuller hadn't made his appearance there a priority.

Davis was fidgeting more than usual and Dominique suspected he wanted to wrap up the interview and get outside to have a cigarette.

"Do you know why Dr. Armour didn't go?" Davis grumbled impatiently.

Ogden shrugged. "I suppose his wife wouldn't let him. They were having a big group at their house for a barbeque that day."

It was obvious that even though Dr. Ogden knew about the party, he hadn't been invited and was more indication that the men weren't really all that close. In any case, it also corroborated Dr. Armour's story. "What happened at the protest?"

"There was a lot of shouting from the greenies."

"What did Mr. Hollis do?"

Ogden took an antacid out of his pocket, unwrapped

it, and popped it into his mouth. So much for being able to help Captain Jaeger get off the stuff, Dominique thought. "He told them he had the best intentions and was going to improve the ratables in this town and bring up the tax base," said Dr. Ogden. "Homeowners wouldn't have their taxes raised and there wouldn't be any overcrowding in the schools or congestion on the roads."

"Did he have any basis for those promises?" Dominique asked.

Dr. Ogden's mouth twitched. "Are you asking me if he was lying? How should I know? That's what he told me and our golf partners when he wanted us to invest— no problems for the environment, water tables, roads, schools"—he paused—"police department or whatever."

"What did the protesters say to his claims?"

"They listened for a while, argued with him, and finally shouted him down. There wasn't anything we could do at that point, so I left." He lowered his head. "I guess he did, too," he added quietly, looking up at the detectives for confirmation.

"What do you mean by that?" said Davis.

"He was found in the quarry. He evidently left the park before he got up there."

Dominique studied the doctor, and couldn't help noticing a slight tremor in his hands. "How do you suppose he got up there?"

"Maybe he walked."

"You don't think he walked up that huge hill to the quarry, do you?"

Dr. Ogden laughed nervously. "Not really. He was

always the first guy to get a golf cart. He didn't walk anywhere if he didn't have to. Are you sure he didn't take his car?"

"His car was found in a parking lot near the park."

Dominique looked closely at the doctor. "Someone gave him a ride. And we don't think it was directly to the Ferrys." The police had found several cigarette butts of Keith Hollis's brand in the grass near the fence in the school yard that overlooked the quarry and they did not show signs of weathering. "We also found some tire tracks from a sports car."

Looking like a deer caught in the headlights, Dr. Ogden slumped in his chair. "I was beginning to have doubts about the investment. He wanted to show me how the water that has collected there would leave without flooding and how the one road leading into the quarry could be widened to make it safer."

"So you went up there to look? What time?"

"I'm not sure. But it was still light out. Light enough to see."

Davis stood up as if he was ready to make an arrest. Dominique hurried to ask her next question. "And you stood on Mr. Ferry's back lawn to look into the quarry?"

A quizzical look knitted Dr. Ogden's eyebrows. "Gabe Ferry's? No. Why would we go there?"

An exasperated noise escaped from Davis's lips. "So where did you go to view into the quarry?" His tone was all sarcasm.

"Where? The back of the school yard. It overlooks the quarry and you can see almost all of it from there."

Dominique had to agree. The view there was almost as good as at Gabriel Ferry's house, and it was far safer to stand there, where there was a twelve-foot chain-link fence set in cement, as compared to no fence on the ragged edge of the cliff. "What did you do next?" she asked.

"He smoked a few cigarettes while he told me all about his big plans for the quarry. It was interesting but I'd heard it all before. Then I looked at my watch and said I had to go back to the fireworks. My boys were meeting me there and I didn't want to disappoint them. It was their last night home before sleep away camp."

"What time was it then?"

"Nine. And the fireworks always start at nine-fifteen."

Davis snorted. "So you left Mr. Hollis up there with no ride?"

"He said he'd get a ride. That I should just leave him there and he'd call on his cell phone for one. He turned his back on me and I left. That was the last I saw him."

"Who was he going to call?"

"I don't know. Can't you figure that out from his cell phone information?"

Dominique couldn't tell this witness that the cell phone had been used to call information for a Grosvenor number at nine-fourteen, but that the name of the number being requested hadn't been given before the connection was disconnected. The police were using that as a parameter for the time of the attack on the victim. Either Mr. Hollis had hung up because the person whose number he wanted had arrived, or because he was interrupted by someone else and voluntarily terminated the information request, or because he was sailing over the top of the cliff. In any event, his phone was found smashed beyond repair and there was no other information available from the server.

"We haven't so far," said Dominique. "When you left, was Mr. Hollis still standing in the school yard?"

"I think so. He was still looking down into the quarry when I turned my car around. After that, I couldn't tell you."

"And he didn't say at all who he was meeting?" Davis asked.

"I told you, no."

Based on the need for directory information, Dominique wasn't at all sure that Hollis was even calling the person he said would pick him up. It seemed to her that he'd know the phone number of whoever that might be, or at least have it programmed into his phone. Unfortunately, they hadn't been able to determine whose phone numbers Hollis had stored on his phone.

"How far is it from the school yard to Gabriel Ferry's, would you say?" Dominique asked the doctor. She knew the answer to that—less than a two-minute walk. There were at least fourteen minutes between the time J.J. Ogden left Keith Hollis in the school yard and the time he was hit over the head at the Ferrys' residence.

He furrowed his brow. "I'm not sure. I don't know his address."

Dominique asked him the question she had asked each of the other doctors. "Do you know Izmir Fakhouri?"

"Yes."

"Is he a friend of yours?"

"Not really. What does he have to do with this?"

"Keith Hollis was living in the same house as Dr. Fakhouri."

"Sorry. I don't know anything about that." It was the same answer Dominique had received twice before. Keith Hollis's life had been compartmentalized, with no carryover from one group to another and no close ties to anyone. But still someone had been angry enough to kill him.

Chapter Nine

Rachel stopped at the bakery and bought black-and-white cookies to bring to Tori's house. The huge chocolate and white frosted cookies were far too big for one person to eat, but she bought four anyway.

Although the street where Tori lived didn't even exist until just four years earlier, Rachel was able to find it. It led steeply up the side of the hill, and each house was built at a completely different altitude, all the way to the top. Each home, from bottom to top, was larger than the previous one. Rachel couldn't help gawking, wide-eyed, for a moment. The term McMansions came to mind.

Tori Hollis lived in the second house from the top. Day lilies brightened a sculptured line of shrubbery fronting the large bay windows on either side of the center hall colonial. A huge window over the ten-foot-high front doors framed an enormous chandelier within. Rachel blinked, hoping to get her eyes back to a normal size, and rang the bell.

Tori and Gracie both answered the door and led Rachel and Jody into the spectacular two-story center hall.

"Lunch will be a few more minutes," Tori said. "Do you want to take a little tour first?"

"We'd love to," Rachel said, speaking both for herself and Jody, whom she was sure couldn't have cared less. Ever since she'd stepped through the doorway, the air conditioning had been reviving Rachel's flagging, nearly nine-month-pregnant energy and now her natural curiosity needed satisfaction.

Tori started with the living room, just off the foyer. Overstuffed couches, chairs and ottomans, all in either large floral or bold stripes, were atop what Rachel was sure were expensive Persian rugs. Mahogany tables and an eight-foot armoire, which reached nearly to the ten-foot ceiling, seemed enhanced by the deep red of the walls. Complementary window treatments hung at the front bay window and the rear French doors leading to a deck which abounded with planters filled with annuals.

Tori next led them into a library, filled floor to ceiling with books, that had a small, portable spiral staircase in front of one of the bookcases. Jody seemed to like that and went to climb it.

"Gracie does that all the time," Tori said, laughing.

"I always wanted one of those," Rachel confided. Too bad it would have been a ridiculous item in her family's cramped house. Tori's living room was bigger than their whole first floor.

Tori went down a hallway past a bathroom with a full

shower and bath and many closets. Rachel understood why they were there when Tori opened a door that led outside to the deck and the pool.

Because the house was built into the hillside, the pool was cantilevered over the disappearing slope. There was a barbeque and outdoor table area off to one side of the large deck surrounding the pool, next to another doorway.

They went back into the house through that door and into the kitchen. Rachel had to hold her breath to keep from gasping.

The kitchen might have come out of the finest of design magazines. Every detail, from the way the color of the cabinets worked with the granite countertop and backsplash tiles, to the insets that seemed custom designed to show off some of Tori's beautiful vases and bowls, to the extra sink on the center island, was magnificent.

"This is gorgeous," Rachel said. "Your designer is brilliant."

Tori beamed. "I am the designer. I planned every inch of this kitchen." She went on to explain the reason for each of the details, and the origin of the items she displayed.

Rachel was struck by how important it all seemed to Tori. For herself, she would have liked a new kitchen, but the old one was fine. Even if she were planning a new one, it would be far more basic than this one. And that wouldn't be for quite some time, until she went back to work full-time at her job as a psychologist.

"Lunch is served," Tori said, pulling salads out of a

special chilling section in her built-in refrigerator. Rachel helped, taking two herself, and following Tori into the dining room.

It was breathtakingly beautiful, with a large upholstered window seat under a bay window with matching Roman shades. The furniture was quite large, so large, in fact, that it would never have even fit into Rachel's dining room. She couldn't imagine it would fit into too many other houses either. She began to have a sense of it all being just a bit too much.

The china on the table was from the same set as the china in the breakfront. Rachel, who had never considered using the china she received for her wedding to serve anyone under the age of eighteen, cringed at the thought of the two preschoolers eating from Tori's set.

But she soon got over her fears, and tendency to compare everything to what she had. It just didn't matter. Tori's lunch was delicious, and the girls both gobbled it up. They shared two of the black-and-white cookies before going out to the deck to play in Gracie's playhouse. Rachel was left wishing she was not so enormous. She really would have liked a chance to get inside the little house.

The girls played well together and Rachel sat on the deck sipping iced tea and talking with Tori. Although they discussed other things, such as the other girls in their former crowd, the subject of the house kept coming up. Tori detailed for Rachel how she decorated each room in the house. It all seemed so important that Rachel was left wondering if Tori was dwelling on the decorating process so much because of her love of her house or maybe because of Keith's loss. But Rachel lived by her rule of never trying to analyze someone's problems unless asked. That restraint was something, she reflected, that her mother would never consider.

Not that Rachel thought her mother was wrong for nosing around the way she did. She'd long ago recognized that what some people might consider to be her mother's meddling in other's business was done with the best of intentions. Wally Morris, who had a really big heart, just wanted to see how she could help and believed it important to understand the complete nature of someone's problems in order to do that. She wasn't a snoop, or a know-it-all, but she was thorough, and she got results.

Rachel was brought out of her reverie by Tori bringing more iced tea for the adults and lemonade for the girls. Rachel couldn't think of a nicer way for her daughter to spend the sunny July afternoon.

Rachel didn't come back from Tori's and Gracie's house until almost four o'clock. By that time, Jody was limp with exhaustion. Rachel tucked Jody into her bed in Rachel's old room even though it meant completely messing up her schedule.

Wally knew something was up. Her normally somewhat rigid daughter would rarely let Jody take such a late nap and would do almost anything to keep her awake so she could go to sleep at her regular time. Yet here Jody was, taking a nap with her mother's full approval.

"How was your lunch?" Wally asked, when Rachel plopped herself down in a chair opposite her. She handed her daughter a glass of milk.

A cloud passed over Rachel's eyes. She was such a pretty young woman, not blond and sunny like her sister, Debbie, whose green eyes always held a trace of humor. Rachel's beauty was of the darker type, quiet, reserved, with her dark eyes and hair. It matched her personality. Rachel was steady, if occasionally inflexible, and warm and forgiving. Right at that moment, though, something was bothering her.

"Tori is nice," she said, "although I gather she doesn't have many friends around here. And her daughter is sweet. She and Jody had a good time."

"So what did you do?"

Rachel filled her in on the afternoon's activities. "And we took the girls into the shallow end of the pool," she concluded.

"She has a full-size pool? Then why does she go down to the public pool?"

"Keith cancelled their country club membership so now they go to the town pool to meet people, for her and for Gracie."

"That makes sense," Wally said. "So what was wrong?"

"Nothing. Why do you think something was wrong?"

Wally said nothing. Explaining her reasoning would get them nowhere. She just had to let whatever it was on Rachel's mind come out on its own.

"Her house is lovely," Rachel said, after taking a sip of her milk. "Every square inch is decorated to perfection. Tori did a lot of the designing on her own."

"It must be hard on her to have to leave the house."

Rachel stared wide-eyed at Wally. "Didn't you know

she doesn't have to move? Since Keith died, the sale can't go through."

"Oh, yes, that's right. Well, that must be some comfort to her," Wally said. "This has to be such a difficult time."

"Yes."

"But how will she afford it? She isn't working, is she?"

"For one thing, she's planning to find a job. In interior decorating. She will probably be a great success. For another, apparently Keith made a big down payment, and since he was the builder, he purchased the house at cost. Plus, you remember Tori comes from money." Rachel frowned and picked up her glass.

There was more to it, Wally could tell. She took a sip of her iced coffee and waited.

"She really loves the house," Rachel said. "She is so proud of it, and every detail is so important."

Wally nodded.

"It almost seemed to be more important than Gracie, or Keith. It was as if, oh, Keith's dead, but thank God I get to keep the house. As if life would have no meaning if she couldn't."

"She may be compensating," Wally observed.

Rachel gave Wally a look that said she understood that, obviously, and wasn't she the one who was a licensed psychologist? "I've considered that."

"And what did you conclude?" Wally said, without acknowledging the look.

"Nothing. I don't know."

Wally took a long look at her daughter and saw a troubled woman. "What do you think it is?" She stopped, suddenly considering a possibility. "Are you wondering whether she wanted to keep the house so much that she killed Keith over it?"

Wally knew Rachel was a sensible person, as well as an intelligent one. Maybe she was seeing something no one else had. She worked with people's personal problems for a living and she was astute. Maybe there was more she could learn about Keith.

"Are you planning to spend more time with her this week?" Wally asked. "Maybe call some of the other girls who are still in town?"

Rachel caught her mother's meaning and frowned. "You want me to pump her for information and repeat it to you?"

Wally had the sense that she was being chastised by her daughter, however subtly. "No, I'm not asking you to betray confidences. And I don't think you have the stomach to pump a person. It could be fun though, and maybe help Tori. You'll be going home soon, but if she reestablishes some relationships with old friends, maybe she won't be so lonely."

Not looking particularly convinced, Rachel said, "I could try. You're right, it could be fun. And I wouldn't mind seeing her again this week."

Wally got an idea. "I think I'd like to have a play date for Jody and her new friend. And maybe you and Tori would like to spend an afternoon together without the kids, out of her house." Wally didn't add that the reason she stressed the meeting outside of Tori's beloved house was that she hoped that Tori would be less focused on it and more honest about her feelings, some of which Rachel might possibly divulge to her mother and some which might even be clues to whoever killed the young woman's husband. "Do you think you could figure something out?"

"Why of course I can. This baby is coming in just a few weeks and there are millions of things I need to buy. I'll call her tonight and set it up. And I'll see if anyone wants to meet us for lunch."

"Thank you for meeting us here," said Dominique when she and Ryan arrived at the offices of the Keith Hollis Group to interview Gigi, Hollis's secretary. She had just returned from her two-week honeymoon in the Canadian Rockies.

"I still can't believe it," she said, biting her lip. She had been crying, Dominique noted, and her wide, blue eyes were rimmed in red. It made her look even younger than what Dominique estimated was about twenty-one.

"My mother left me a message on our answering machine," Gigi continued, reaching for a tissue. Her new wedding band shone in the light from the window of the rather small office behind her desk, where Keith Hollis had conducted his business.

The office had been thoroughly searched the same day as the body was discovered, and subsequently sealed. There hadn't been any way to get in touch with Gigi for questioning, until now. She had called the police herself, as soon as she received the message.

"I know this is a shock," said Dominique. "But we need your help. Can you think of anyone at all who might have wanted to kill Mr. Hollis?"

Gigi rolled her eyes. Both Dominique and Ryan looked at each other.

"Were there a lot of people who were angry with Mr. Hollis?" Ryan asked. Dominique got the sense that he was itching to write down a list, pick a likely candidate, and wrap up the case. She, however, didn't think it would be so easy. From what she had discovered already, Gigi hadn't been employed there long.

"Mr. Hollis spent a lot of time on the phone, and he yelled a lot. I didn't always know who he was talking to, because he placed most of the calls, but I do know that the people who are listed as his partners were some of the ones he yelled at."

"Can you remember what was said?"

"You'll get your stinkin' money," Gigi said.

Ryan's brow furrowed. "I beg your pardon?"

"That's what he said. Only he said it really loud."

"Is that all?" asked Ryan, looking like he wanted to run right out and get all the phone records for every day since Gigi started working.

"No. Sometimes he yelled that things had better get done on time or else. And he slammed his phone down a lot."

Dominique had already noticed that. The plastic on the receiver of Hollis's phone was so battered it had cracked. She mentioned that to Gigi.

"And that's the second replacement since I got here."

"How long ago did you start?" asked Dominique.

"About six months ago. Right after I graduated from college. I did it in three and a half years," she added proudly.

Dominique wondered if there was something to her having been there only six months. "Do you know why the last secretary left?"

"No."

"Can you get us her name?"

"Sure." She tapped a few keys, looked at her computer screen, and wrote down the information.

Ryan had been quiet for a while. "You finished college and you took a job as a secretary?" he said. Once he'd said it he seemed to realize that it might seem like an insulting question, especially the way he'd asked it, and his face flushed red.

Dominique was used to the flushes. With Ryan's red hair and associated coloring, and his tendency to speak before he thought things through, it happened often.

"Have you tried to get a job in this economy? When I was in high school the job market was wide open, people getting signing bonuses, the whole nine yards. Now most of the people who graduated with me are lounging on their parents' couches. I felt lucky to have this job."

Ryan looked like he had been laid to waste. "I apologize. It's just that—"

"Don't worry about it. I'll get something better." Suddenly she got a strange look on her face. "I guess I have to start looking right away."

"Before you do that," Dominique said, hoping to get the interview back on track, "we need a list of all his meetings."

"I can get that from his computer," Gigi said, rising to go into the inner office.

"That's already been done," Ryan told her. "What my partner wants is meetings that were off the schedule."

"Like when someone dropped in?"

"Did you keep records?"

"Not for personal friends or relatives. But yes, if someone stopped by, Mr. Hollis always had me write it down, so he could remember to mention it the next time he saw the person." She looked at her record book. "I'll make you a copy," she said, and then she burst into tears again.

It must have been a slow news day because B. J. Waters and her noon news team were seen in Grosvenor questioning everyone from the mayor to the police chief to Georgia Dewey, whose comments seemed to have been edited. "I always knew something would happen," she said. "When people live like—" The rest of what she said was inaudible, but Wally could still see her mouth moving. Unfortunately, or maybe not, she couldn't read lips.

B. J. set up outside the pharmacy, where she proclaimed it to be the place of employment of the murder victim's niece. While no one from within made a statement, viewers knew that B. J. was doing her job, being on location, and getting out the news, even though absolutely nothing new about the case was reported. Viewers were left with the sense that the newspeople were more than a little annoyed at the police force's lack of results.

But it gave Wally an idea. "Louise," she said, when she'd reached her friend on her cell phone, "what do you think the chances are of us talking to Fiona's mom about her brother?"

"I'll get Norman to ask her."

It didn't take long for Louise to call back. "I'm in your driveway and we are going over to Peggy's house right now."

Wally barely had time to package up her latest batch of blueberry muffins in a pretty basket. She couldn't arrive empty-handed.

Louise had obviously thought along the same lines, but had stopped at the bakery. "She said she'd be happy to talk to us. She really wants us to understand her poor brother." She took her eyes off the road long enough to look at Wally. "Peggy is a darling woman," Louise said. "I don't want her to be hurt any more than she has been."

"I'm not planning to accuse her of anything," Wally promised. "I just think she may have some information about Keith that the police didn't think to ask."

Peggy lived in a garden apartment across from the hospital. "I moved out of Grosvenor years ago," she explained while making a pot of coffee. "As soon as Fiona finished school. I just couldn't afford the taxes any more."

It was a familiar phrase and one that backers of the building in the quarry had used to try to garner more support. Any new ratables would have to take the pressure off those with limited means or fixed incomes. Those in opposition were quick to point out that new houses would mean more children in the schools and greater demand for municipal services that would surely negate any gains.

"It was a struggle those last two years Fiona was in high school. My job just doesn't pay enough for us to live in Grosvenor."

Louise had explained that Peggy was a physical therapist.

"I took Keith in when our dad died. Our mom died years before and it was just Keith and Dad living alone in Newark. He was only fifteen, my baby brother. I got him enrolled in school and he got involved in sports. Soon he had a whole new life." She was smiling, though her eyes glittered with moisture.

"Lucky kid," Louise said.

Peggy had been setting out plates, napkins, and silverware, but she stopped to look up at Louise. "No, I was the one who was lucky. Without Keith's kidney, I would have died. He ended up going to community college instead of a big football school because of me." She shook her head, allowing her tears to fall.

"But he did okay. He had a good life until . . ."

Wally felt uncomfortable in the presence of so much grief. "I know you did everything you could for him. Louise told me about it." She had done far more, according to Louise, on occasion hiring lawyers to keep her brother out of jail and in school.

Peggy nodded. "I just did what I thought was right. Keith had a hard life before he came to live with me. How could anyone expect him to be perfect?"

Louise nodded agreement. "Didn't you tell me that some of the boys he was running around with here were a wild bunch?"

"They were, but at least two of them settled down

and made something of themselves. I was proud of my brother." She dried her eyes. "I thought he would be okay. He had a job, a marriage, and then the twins. They are really sweet girls, even with that shrew of a mother."

Wally bit her lip. She'd heard people's opinions of Merle before.

"And you can't blame Keith for leaving that woman. He was still a good father." A shakiness in her voice made Wally look at her more closely and led her to realize that Peggy didn't really believe what she had just said.

The coffee was ready and the women sat down at the kitchen table. Wally's blueberry muffins were a hit and the gooey, sticky, yummy coffee ring that Louise had bought made Wally lose her resolve to restrict calories. She decided to have her coffee black, just to atone.

The mood relaxed a bit and Wally ventured another question. "I was hoping you could help us figure out a few things that have puzzled the police," she said, trying to choose her words carefully. "Someone was angry at Keith, so angry that he was killed. Who might have been so angry?"

Peggy stared wide-eyed at Wally. "I can't imagine being that angry at anyone, can you?"

It was a question Wally had asked herself several times over the past few years and been unable to understand. "No. I really can't. But someone was."

"Of all the people I knew who had something to do with Keith, I can't imagine anyone. Not even Merle. Not even Tori, even though he had left her and sold the house she loved more than life itself."

Wally noted that Peggy had the same opinion of Tori's attachment to the house that she did. "What about his male friends?"

"I only know one, J.J. Ogden. He went to school with Keith." She grimaced. "He got a football scholarship and a good education."

They didn't seem to be getting anywhere so Wally tried a new line of questioning. "I wondered why Keith bought the quarry in the first place, since initially it didn't seem as if he'd planned to build anything or even change what was there." There had been a two-year gap between the time Keith contracted to buy the quarry from Bucky Ralston and the time he started making plans to build there.

Peggy seemed to have given the subject a great deal of thought. "I think it's because of our dad. He used to work in the quarry, as a laborer. Our family had to really struggle. And when Dad died, pretty young, there were no medical benefits. Keith said he wanted to get them back for killing Dad. Owning the quarry might have made him feel as if he put one over on them."

"Who?"

"The Ralstons."

"That's so sad," Louise said.

"But he became friendly with Bucky Ralston," Wally said.

"I think he did that to show how far he had come. I don't think he ever liked the man."

"Was there any trouble with the sale?"

Peggy shook her head. "I don't know. We never talked about his business. The only thing I knew was that he needed more money, since one of his big backers was pulling out. I couldn't help him though." She seemed so sorry that she couldn't help, but Wally could tell that Louise was outraged that Keith would even ask this woman who was struggling to make ends meet to help him with his venture.

There was an awkward silence. No suitable response to Peggy's sadness seemed appropriate.

"Look," she said, "I'm not blind. I know that Keith had some bad qualities. He could be one of the nicest guys in the world, keep any secret if asked, but if he were threatened, he'd go for a person's Achilles' heel. He'd say or do whatever he could to get what he wanted, even reveal secrets he'd promised to keep, and there were people who hated him for it." An awkward silence followed, allowing her words to linger in the air. Wally couldn't help but wonder whose secrets he might have divulged.

She was brought back to the present by Peggy. "Will you be able to help the police find my brother's killer?" she finally asked.

Wally sincerely doubted it, more every day. But she was confident that the police would find out who killed Keith, and she told Peggy so.

After thanking Louise and Wally for the goodies and the visit, Peggy looked happier than when they first arrived. Wally hoped things would get easier for her soon.

Chapter Ten

Wally hurried into the kitchen to see why Sammy was barking. Rachel and Jody were upstairs taking a mid-morning nap and she didn't want to wake them.

Ordinarily a quiet dog, the Labrador retriever had one button, a dog in the yard, which, when pushed, guaranteed he'd violate his no barking training. He never barked at squirrels, chipmunks, birds, or occasional skunks or possums, schoolchildren cutting through on their way home, or even the increasing number of deer that traipsed between the barn and house. But if a dog showed up, Sammy broadcast the infringement on his territory.

"Let's go see who it is," said Wally. She took a leash off the hook and headed outside.

The dog, a Gordon setter, waited patiently for them to approach, then, just as Wally and Sammy got close, dropped his front defensively. Sammy's back was

ridged and his tail straight up and Wally began to wonder whether she should have ordered Sammy to stay in
the house. But then both dogs touched noses and exchanged other kinds of doggie greetings.

"Manners, boys," Wally said, as she clipped the leash
on the visitor. Sammy and the other dog continued to
get acquainted while Wally read his tag.

"Well, hello, Omega. Hold still while I get your
phone number so I can call your family." Wishing she
had thought to bring her reading glasses, she strained to
look at the numbers.

"Oh," she said when she realized what the family
name was. "You have certainly been traveling around,
haven't you? Gabe must be worried sick."

She hooked the leash onto a pole and went inside to
get the portable phone. She had already dialed by the
time she came back out to stay with the dog, and she
had a bowl of water in her other hand.

The phone was answered on the first ring, leading
Wally to conclude the Ferrys were not unaware of their
missing pet. Gabe promised to come right down to pick
up Omega.

Wally changed the leash that she was using for
Omega to a twenty-five-foot anchored lead so she could
throw tennis balls for the two dogs and keep them occupied. Both dogs were beginning to tire by the time
Gabe Ferry arrived.

He was wearing a navy St. Michael's College baseball cap and matching T-shirt which showed off his
well-toned physique. Wally briefly thought how much
Louise would have liked to be there, especially since

Gabe also wore cargo shorts and Tevas. "I can't believe he traveled this far," said Gabe, giving Omega a big hug and Sammy a pat on the head. "I clocked it on the way over. It's almost two miles."

Both dogs panted happily and took turns draining the water bowl that Wally kept refilling. It seemed a shame to break up the party, so Wally offered Gabe some lemonade.

"We've taken up enough of your time," Gabe said, but he followed Wally into the house anyway.

"It was no problem. We get a lot of four-footed visitors, but they usually live in the neighborhood." She poured out two glasses. "Does Omega often set off on his own?"

Gabe shook his head. "It's only been a problem since the fences are down for the repair work on the cliff. We've tried keeping him inside, but since he's used to spending time outside whenever he wants, it's been hard. I let him out this morning before breakfast and he just took off."

"Poor guy. He didn't eat today?"

"Actually, he had already eaten. Petra was up earlier and fed him. I didn't know."

"So since Omega wasn't motivated by his empty stomach to come back inside, he left on his own?"

"I didn't realize it at first, since he usually comes right back in. And I guess I got distracted."

He pointed to the headline of the local paper which read: MURDERER OF KEITH COLLINS STILL AT LARGE."

"I see they got the name wrong," Wally observed. It was nothing new.

"They got my name right and my address, too. Not that it matters. We have a regular stream of sightseers coming to look at the scene of the crime. A number of them are former students of mine."

Wally sensed opportunity knocking. "That must be so hard."

Gabe nodded. "It's embarrassing. We didn't do anything wrong, but we look like we killed Keith."

"Do you have any idea why he was on your property?"

The expression on Gabe's face told Wally he had wracked his brain and come up with nothing. "I don't know," he said. "During the campaign for town council I had made a point of avoiding a confrontation with Keith if we weren't in a public place because he tended to lie about what I actually said." He paled. "Oh, no. That almost makes it sound as if I had a grudge against him."

"Not at all. More like you were protecting yourself."

Gabe nodded. "You've got that right. He twists, er, twisted, everything I said. When I said that building in the quarry wouldn't be good for the community, he told people I said it would ruin my view and lower my property value. When I disagreed with his redevelopment plans for the downtown area, he said I was in favor of bringing in several fast food chains. That couldn't be further from the truth."

Wally had heard both those things. She had no opinion about their validity either way, but the man sitting before her sounded sincere.

"The police talked to me for hours," Gabe continued. "They wanted to know everything, about when I saw him the last time, what was said, what had gone on in the past. They asked about the rest of my family, too. It seems like we are all under investigation."

Wally couldn't imagine that. It made her uncomfortable to even contemplate the thought. "I guess you'll feel a lot better when they catch whoever did it," she said, failing to find a better comment.

"So far it doesn't look like they are doing anything to find the murderer," Gabe said, "at least to me."

"You never know," Wally said lightly. "Just as they asked you where you were at the time, I'm sure they asked all the other susp—" She could have swallowed her lips.

Gabe scowled. "I was at the Nortons. On their deck. I go there every year for a barbeque and to watch the fireworks."

"I'm not asking—"

"I'm telling you what I told the police," Gabe said, his voice rising. "That's where I was at the time of the murder. With friends."

"Okay." Wally wondered why he was making a point of stressing that he was there. "I'm sure the police have verified it," she said, soothingly.

Gabe scowled. "They haven't."

"Why not?"

"Those friends left town the next morning for a cruise, before the body was found. They haven't been reached yet. But I'm told the police are still trying to get a call through." His face darkened. "It's so embarrassing."

Wally thought about her own friends who had left town for a safari in Africa. They weren't back either and she wondered how hard they would be to reach, if necessary. "But your wife can verify it, so that doesn't matter. Right?"

"No. She was out of town on her yearly retreat. She goes to the Chautauqua Institution for two weeks from late June to early July with a group of fellow writers. The kids are in camp for the summer. I was on my own that night."

"Then at least no one should be bothering your family." She finished off her lemonade. "When are your friends coming back?"

"You think I'm in trouble, right? I don't know. And I don't know how to find out."

"The police will do what they can. Try to keep calm." But when she brought his empty glass over to the sink she wondered how that would be possible. Still, she put on a brave face for him and waved as he took Omega home.

While Sammy settled down for a well earned nap, Wally took a look at the rest of the local newspaper. There was coverage of the Fourth of July parade and the winners of the various holiday contests were listed. A story about what was going on at the town's summer programs had pictures beneath the story and Wally couldn't help wondering, from past experience, how many of the names in the captions were wrong. She turned to the Letters to the Editor. Once again there was a letter from Kelley Peren and Wally read it with renewed interest. But while she expected Kelley to show an I-told-you-so attitude, she was surprised to see that the letter was really no different in tone or content than all the others. It was as if Kelley didn't know that Keith had fallen to the bottom of the quarry from one of the unprotected cliffs. An editor's note after the letter briefly mentioned Keith's fall.

The only conclusion Wally could draw was that the paper had printed an old letter, as much as their policy was to never do that. One had to submit a letter to the editor by the beginning of the week in order for it to appear, and any letters not printed were discarded. Yet this seemingly out of date letter had been printed. So much for policy. Their little note after the out-of-date letter only emphasized their mistake.

Rachel still looked groggy when she came into the kitchen carrying Jody. The little girl's face was bright red from the heat and she lay limply against her mother.

"Let's get you something to drink," said Wally, taking Jody and sitting her at the table. She put a glass of apple juice in front of her granddaughter and handed Rachel a glass of milk.

Between the liquid refreshment and the cool of the air conditioned kitchen, they both soon revived.

"I should have put the air conditioner on," Rachel said. "The sun moved and came right in to beat down on us." She took another sip of her milk and, making sure Jody wasn't looking, made a face. Wally had seen her do that before. But she needed her calcium, so there was no avoiding it. "I thought I heard someone down here before. Is Dad home already?"

"No, and I wasn't talking to myself either. Gabriel Ferry was here to pick up his dog."

"Why?"

Wally explained what happened and filled Rachel in on the conversation. "And I'd guess he is a suspect, at least. Even if there are stronger candidates."

"Like who?"

"I don't know. I can't really get a sense of what's going on."

Rachel nodded. "I'm sure you can figure out something," she said. "I have confidence in you." She reached for the newspaper. "Is there anything interesting in here?" She skimmed the Letters to the Editor page. "Who is Kelley Peren?"

Wally told her about the woman who had nearly fallen into the quarry while trying to get her cat out of a tree on an inadequately fenced stretch of the rim. "She's been writing these letters every few weeks since then. But obviously she doesn't keep up with the news or they are printing old letters."

"Kelley Peren," Rachel repeated. "I knew someone with that name in high school. But I would think she'd be married by now."

"Maybe she didn't change her name."

"Maybe, but she sure changed something. Kelley Peren couldn't have written cogent sentences if her life depended on it, at least not when I knew her."

"That's not a nice thing to say," Wally said.

"I tutored her in English for a whole year. I know what I'm talking about."

"Maybe you were better at it than you thought," Wally said, giggling.

"She was an incredible artist though, with a great

sense of style," Rachel said, reminiscing. "Too bad she could never tutor me in drawing."

Wally, whose own efforts at art were on a par with those of her nursery school class, understood her daughter's wistfulness.

Chapter Eleven

Dominique found herself getting jittery just watching Davis, the county detective whose job she'd just love to have, as they waited for Bucky Ralston to answer the door. He stood on the front steps of the huge house in the old section of town where the late-nineteenth and early-twentieth century moguls from New York used to have their summer homes. Not cottages, by any stretch of the imagination, unless one were using the terminology of Newport, Rhode Island, albeit on a lesser scale. This was the neighborhood in which the proposed Dolores Hampton Museum would be, if Grosvenor was lucky enough to win the contest. Dominique wasn't sure which of the houses it would be in, because more than one was in need of extensive repairs.

These houses, from what Dominique had heard, had eight to ten bedrooms, staff quarters, sometimes even an elevator, and on a few, carriage height blocks were attached to the parts of their wide porches that bordered the driveway, presumably so that the ladies of the manor could step into their carriages without having to climb up steps.

Unlike some of the Victorian, Tudor, and Georgian houses surrounding it, whose intricate paint jobs using authentic, nineteenth-century colors had enhanced every elaborate detail on the houses, the Ralstons' house was painted cadet blue with white trim. It did look newer than the other houses. It was probably not more than ninety years old and it was a center-hall colonial. But it was just as big as the others.

Davis lit another cigarette. He had stepped on the last one he'd finished and then tossed it into the shrubbery surrounding the front of the house, with a "they'll never notice" look on his face. That was probably true, as the landscaping was thick and the underplantings were completely filled in. There was a lovely mix of annual and perennial flowers lining the walks and flower beds. It was probably gorgeous here in the spring, Dominique thought, with the azaleas, mountain laurel, rhododendron, cherry blossoms and dogwood all in bloom. One of the Ralstons seemed to be an avid gardener.

The door opened and Davis hastily put out his cigarette, this time placing the butt in his pocket after stubbing it out. "Mr. Ralston?" Davis asked the tall, somewhat soft-looking man.

Bucky Ralston looked as if he'd just come back from playing golf and having several beverages at the nineteenth hole. His white slacks were crisply pleated, as was the button-down awning-striped shirt he wore. He had white bucks on his feet and the comb marks in his thinning hair were still visible. He was probably in his early sixties, Dominique estimated.

"Can I help you?" Ralston asked.

Davis introduced the two of them and explained why they were there, effectively taking over the whole interview himself. It wasn't the first time that had happened, and Dominique knew it wouldn't be the last. But she also knew that if she had something that needed to be asked, Davis would, at least after a while, defer to her.

Ralston invited them inside. "Gretchen isn't home," he said. "But can I offer you something to drink?" He led them into a room off the large foyer and headed over to a table on which several decanters and a pitcher of ice water were displayed. Dominique had only seen that on television or in the movies and wondered if this man had provided the ice water himself or if he had servants to do that for him.

"Water please," Davis replied. Dominique indicated she would like some, too. Ralston handed them their drinks and poured himself a martini he'd already mixed. They all took seats on the large sofas near the fireplace.

"Mr. Ralston," Davis said, "we are here investigating Keith Hollis's death at the quarry and we'd like your help."

"Okay."

"I understand that you sold the quarry to Mr. Hollis a few years ago."

"Yes. We had stopped mining about fifteen years earlier and I decided it was time to let it go. It had been my
father's, you know."

Dominique did. She had done a lot of research in the
past few days and knew that the quarry started blasting
in the twenties and continued until the mid-seventies,
until one blast caused a fault line in the rock to split and
tons of water flooded the basements of the houses down
the mountain below the quarry. Lawsuits had deci-
mated the assets of the business, even though they continued removing rock for years, every bit they could get
without having to blast again.

She also knew that the houses surrounding the area
had suffered structural damage from the percussion of
the blasts, which had taken place at precisely ten minutes to three, weekdays. The blasts themselves were
strong enough, it was said, to knock someone out of
bed and damage the crystal in a cabinet. Dominique
had been in the home of a friend who had bought one
of those old houses. When she and James helped their
friends re-wallpaper a room they had uncovered a six-
foot–long crack.

Restrictive signs had been erected on the street corners of most of the roads leading down the hill from the
quarry, stating weight limits of vehicles intending to
drive down them. Before that, trucks full of the basalt
from the quarry drove down any street they liked from
the one entrance to the quarry and filtered into the local
traffic. Their heavy rumblings vibrated the windows of
every home as they passed and terrified mothers of

school children who had to walk along the streets that had no sidewalks.

Eventually, since there could be no more blasting, the quarrying abated. Everyone was glad when the quarry officially closed. Nature ran its course and the open space became filled with grass and small animals, which attracted birds of prey, and eventually trees sprang up and a herd of deer took up residence.

"I tried to buy it back," Ralston added, "when I found out what Keith had planned. But he wouldn't sell."

Dominique had filled Davis in on the highlights of what she'd learned about the quarry war as well as the quarry's history. "When you sold the quarry to Hollis," Davis said, "what did you expect him to do with it?"

A look that could have been anger or could have been remorse came over Ralston's face. "I didn't know. But I didn't expect him to try to build something in there." There was a tension in his voice that Dominique couldn't place. He didn't seem a likely candidate to be a tree-hugger, but he seemed very upset about the prospective building.

Davis snorted. "He was a developer, wasn't he?"

"Yes, that's true. But from what he had told me, he was also interested in preserving open space. That's big in New Jersey, you know. I thought he was looking for a tax break."

Davis grumbled something of an answer. Dominique sensed his politics were for something other than preservation.

"And you were against the building?" Davis said.

"Have you ever seen the quarry? It is beautiful—open and wild and full of life. Keith wanted to pave paradise."

"So you wanted to buy it back to stop him. What would you have done if he'd sold it to you?"

"I would have given it to the township," Ralston said, "to use for a park."

"How generous," Davis said. Dominique, who had been learning more and more about the detective for some time, suspected that Ralston's altruism only annoyed the county employee.

Ralston scowled. "That land is worth a lot of money. Most people would have considered it a generous gift."

Dominique thought it was time to speak up. "I agree, Mr. Ralston. You said Mr. Hollis turned you down when you asked to buy it back?"

"It was such a mistake for me to sell it. And I offered him double what he paid, just so no one would build on the land."

Perhaps a real motive was emerging here, Dominique thought. She could certainly tell that Davis was listening closely. "You are that against the development?"

"Do you have any idea of what it will take? They will have to blast out more rock just to be able to pour foundations. They will have to cut down many of the trees, ruining the habitat for so many creatures, and drain the quarry. It'll be just like any other development, except it'll be in a hole in the ground in the middle of a mountain."

"With high cliffs overlooking it," said Dominique. "And people in houses on the cliffs who will no longer have the open space, greenery and animals to look at. They will just see the roofs of new houses."

Davis leaned forward toward Ralston, who had finished his drink. "That has the residents up there angry, doesn't it?" Dominique knew just which resident Davis had in mind, his favorite suspect, Gabriel Ferry. But Bucky Ralston's answer didn't add anything to Davis's theory.

"So I've heard," said Ralston. His tone implied that he didn't really have much to do with the people who lived near the quarry. "Would either of you care for another drink?" When they declined he poured himself another one.

"Were you one of the environmentalists protesting the development?" Dominique asked.

Ralston shook his head. "No. They wouldn't have me—I was as much the enemy as Hollis, because I sold the land to him. I wasn't aligned with any group."

"But do you know about any of the people who were opposing the quarry? Had you heard anyone threaten to harm Mr. Hollis if he went ahead with his plans?"

"Are you asking me to implicate someone?" Ralston asked. "I'm sorry, but I can't help you."

"One more thing," said Davis. "Could you please tell us your whereabouts on the night of the murder?"

Ralston took a big breath and exhaled. "I was at the fireworks until they finished."

"Any witnesses?"

"My wife, and several other people."

Davis's phone rang and he went outside.

"Please ask your wife to give us a call," said Dominique. "And please call if you think of anything else."

By the time Dominique got outside, Davis was on his toes, practically dancing. Dominique didn't have to wait for him to tell her what had him so excited. "We got him."

"Who?"

"The professor. Gabe Ferry. The one who I thought all along did it."

Dominique ignored his smug attitude. "I thought he had an alibi."

"Well, apparently he didn't," Davis said, in an almost scarily singsong voice.

Sometimes his lack of self control really got to Dominique, and this was one of those times. Wally Morris was convinced that Gabe Ferry wasn't the type to hit a man over the head with a shovel and push him over a cliff. While Dominique knew stranger things had happened, she had been inclined to go along with Wally on her assessment. Now there seemed to be evidence to the contrary.

Davis made a note and then looked up at her, grinning. "We did have confirmation that he was on his friend's deck on the other side of the quarry during the fireworks and for the rest of the evening. But one of the other guests from that evening remembers him going home right after the fireworks ended to check on his dog who he said was frightened by the noise."

"How long was he gone?"

"The guest did not remember when he came back, just that he saw him later on and asked about the dog.

Mr. Ferry told him the dog was fine." Davis lit a cigarette. "It's just as I thought. We don't have to go looking
around for our killer. The man owned the property
where the murder took place. Who else is gonna go
there to kill someone?"

Dominique had never subscribed to that theory, at
least not the basis of it. But they had to find out the
truth. "We'll have to go talk to him again," she said,
getting into her car.

"Right behind you," said Davis, rubbing his hands
together.

They found Gabriel Ferry in his office at the university. The office was cluttered with books, papers, and
magazines. Old photos of Grosvenor, Newark, and
New York covered the walls. On the desk an old child-
sized pail bearing the name of Ralston's quarry held a
variety of pens and pencils and a space had been
cleared where two books by Dr. Ferry sat between a
pair of expensive bookends. A poster for the Dolores
Hampton Museum competition covered the door.

Davis wasted no time confronting the historian with
what they had learned.

"You're right," said Dr. Ferry. "I did leave for a few
minutes. I had to put Omega in a dog crate in the basement because of what he does during fireworks and afterward I wanted to let him out. It's a little small for him."

The explanation made sense to Dominique but she
had the same concerns as Davis, who voiced them.
"Why didn't you tell us this? You realize it kills your alibi, don't you?"

Ferry looked at the detective. "I was just home for a few minutes."

"But that was the approximate time of the murder."

"I thought you said he was killed during the fireworks."

Davis hadn't said anything of the kind, Dominique was sure. But the rumors that were going around carried a shred of truth. The victim had been calling information for the number of a cab company when his call was terminated. It could have been cut off because the victim was hit on the head with a shovel and was falling or being pushed into the quarry. But no one was sure of anything. Although it seemed as if Hollis had lived for a time after the fall, no one was sure of the exact moment of the attack or the death. Davis said that to Ferry.

The man paled. "Look," he said, "I didn't do it." Beads of sweat popped out on his forehead. "You've got to believe me."

Dominique could see that Davis did not. But she had her doubts and she knew she'd better quickly find the real killer, or Gabe Ferry would soon be arrested.

"So," said Louise, coming into the kitchen and reaching for one of the cookies Wally had on a plate, "what's up and why can't we go to the pool this afternoon?"

"Would you like iced coffee with that?" Wally asked, setting out glasses.

"Is it regular or decaf?"

"Half and half."

"Okay," Louise said. "I'll just have to have two glasses."

Wally poured coffee into two glasses filled with ice

and added milk. "We can't go to the pool because we have to babysit."

"Where is Rachel?"

"Upstairs."

"Is she alright?"

"She's fine. Why do you ask?"

"Because you said we have to babysit. I wondered why she wasn't watching Jody herself."

"Oh. Because of the plan."

Louise smiled. "What do you have up your sleeve?"

"Rachel is going shopping with Tori Hollis and then they are meeting a bunch of old friends."

"What's the occasion?"

"Lunch."

"And she isn't bringing Jody because . . . ?"

"Because we are watching both children here. Isn't that nice of us?"

Louise looked to the ceiling for an answer. Failing to find one there, she pointed out to Wally that she could think of a few better things to do with her afternoon.

"I thought you were looking forward to being a grandma," Wally said.

"I am. But not to other people's grandchildren."

"If that's how you feel, I'll do it myself. But you would have to stop eating these cookies."

"I've already had three. It's time for me to stop."

"So you won't join me?"

"No, I will. But you'll have to tell me why we are do- ing this. It's not just so the girls can have some time without the children, right?"

"In a way. They are going to a restaurant for adults,

not Chuck E. Cheese, and they'll have adult conversation with other adults. That's hard to do with two children under the age of four."

Louise cocked her red head to one side. "You're hoping Rachel will find something out, aren't you?"

"It would be nice."

"And you think Rachel is going to grill Tori about the murder? What interrogation method does she plan to use?"

Wally scowled. "You know what I mean. There are several people in this town under suspicion, and a murderer on the loose. The case needs to be solved. I'm just saying that if Rachel finds something out, it could be useful."

"What are we doing while all this sleuthing and eating like adults is going on?" asked Louise.

"We're feeding the children and taking them to the playground."

"This is some way to spend my day off."

"I'll make it up to you," Wally promised. "Have another cookie."

Louise shook her head. "Not yet. A Jag just pulled into your driveway and you should see if Rachel is ready to go. I'll go make chitchat with Tori and see if I can get anything out of her."

Five minutes later Rachel, practically bulging out of her sun dress, was seated in luxury beside Tori and pulling out of the driveway. Wally and Louise got busy entertaining the two preschoolers.

Chapter Twelve

Rachel leaned back into the seat of the air-conditioned car and smiled. She was looking forward to shopping with Tori and seeing their old friends. It hadn't been fifteen years for her as it had been since Tori saw those "girls," but it had been a while. She intended to enjoy herself.

Tori was well dressed for the occasion, wearing a short skirt and sleeveless blouse that showed off her long, toned arms and legs, and strappy designer sandals. Beside her, Rachel felt a bit dowdy, since she was wearing a well-worn maternity dress. But it didn't matter a bit. They were there to have fun.

"Are we buying or just picking things out?" Tori asked.

"Just picking things out." Rachel had inherited her mother's superstitions, handed down over many generations, about bringing home baby clothing or nursery furniture before the baby is born. For that reason,

151

Rachel was going to select all the baby things, in two possible gender choices, and leave them at the store. Once the baby was born, Wally would collect the appropriate set and bring it to Rachel in Westchester.

The two women had fun choosing every item, but Tori became quieter and quieter. Rachel suggested that maybe she could finish another time.

"No, I'm okay, really, I was just remembering how happy I was when I was shopping for Gracie."

"Did you know she'd be a girl?"

"No. All I bought was boy things, since I was really hoping she'd be a boy. That's what Keith wished for. He already had two daughters. But I was delighted when she turned out to be a girl. I called the store and told them exactly what I wanted and my mother returned the rest."

Apparently Tori wasn't burdened by all the superstition. Still, considering that Rachel didn't know whether she'd have a boy or a girl, this was the best solution. And why tempt fate?

"I don't think Adam really cares," said Rachel, realizing that she couldn't know that for sure. The best that could be positively said was that Adam knew what not to say. She paid the deposit for the baby clothes and gave her credit card information to the saleswoman so they would hold the selections in a box marked with her name, as well as Wally's phone number. "Let's go have lunch," she said, longing to get off her feet.

"Good idea. And we'll be right on time." Tori led the way back to the car and pulled out of the parking lot. "That was fun. Especially the part where we shopped for a girl." Rachel agreed, although she could really see putting those boy outfits on someone.

When they had pulled into the parking lot of Xebec's, Rachel heaved herself out of the car. In just a few minutes they were sitting in a booth surrounded by murals of Monet-like landscapes. Three of their old friends came to join them.

Becky came in first. She hadn't changed at all since they graduated from high school. She still wore her light brown hair long and little makeup, but her large blue eyes didn't really need it anyway. Tori had no trouble recognizing her and, while Rachel wouldn't have said they greeted each other as warmly as she and Becky had, the two women seemed happy to get reacquainted.

Nyla, who came in right behind her carrying several bags of shoe boxes, seemed to be out of breath. Her dark, wavy hair was practically plastered to her neck and her face was flushed. "I got here ten minutes early and was just looking in the window of the shoe store next door when a pair of shoes called my name. How could I be so rude as to ignore them? I just had to buy them."

"It looks as if some of their friends were calling you, too," Rachel observed. "It must have been noisy in there."

"Not really," Nyla said, missing Rachel's joke, "but it was hot. The air conditioner was on the blink."

Becky shook her head. "You poor thing. I hope they gave you a good discount." She looked around. "I wonder what's keeping Amy. When I called her office, they said she'd already left."

Nyla giggled. "Maybe we should check the shoe store."

Tori spoke up. "If I'm not mistaken, here she is."

All three women watched as Amy, wearing a light pink linen suit and lime green flip-flops, approached the table. "Maybe you and I should both go to the shoe sale," Nyla said, giggling again and nodding toward Amy's feet.

"I just wear these to run around. Believe me, when I'm in court, my shoes are just as uncomfortable as yours." She picked up her menu. "And we should order because I have to appear again in an hour."

"That's right," said Becky. "I have patients lined up all afternoon. They are already getting their back-to-school physicals."

"Ah," said Nyla, who was a teacher. "The luxury of having the summer off."

The women placed orders for appetizers and entrees, and made preliminary choices for dessert. Today was a day to treat themselves and they would be leaving out no course. While they were waiting for their food, they updated each other on their families. Since no one had heard from Tori in such a long time, the talk soon turned to her. Everyone was so sorry to hear about her misfortune, but that didn't stop the women from asking questions.

Amy took a sip of her iced latte. "Keith's daughters are teenagers, aren't they?"

Tori nodded. "Keith was a lot older than me. And no," she added, looking at Rachel, "I was not the cause of the breakup of his marriage to Merle."

Rachel didn't say anything. She knew that someone

would have to fill the void in the conversation and she hoped it would be Tori.

"That honor goes to none other than Alberta Dellaquan."

Rachel thought she recognized the name. "Of Dellaquan Builders?"

"The same. Keith worked for them when he quit college. One of the brothers went to school with him."

"Was Alberta one of the daughters?" Nyla asked.

"The baby of the family," Tori said, making a face. "She came on to Keith shamelessly, always after him to reach up for this or that in the office, wearing skimpy clothes. I guess he was weak, and gave in. It cost him his marriage and his job."

"But he didn't marry her, he married you," Rachel said.

Tori grimaced. "That doesn't mean he stopped seeing her. I was stupid."

When their appetizers arrived, Becky asked, "Why do you say you were stupid?"

"Because I fell in love with a man who had been divorced for cheating on his wife. Those men don't change, not a bit." She took a sip of wine. "I'm pretty sure he cheated on me, too, with Alberta. And then he had the nerve to say seeing her didn't mean anything."

"Do you have any proof he was cheating again?" Nyla asked.

Tori didn't answer.

"Because maybe you were wrong and you didn't have to break it . . ." She looked around the table, clearly embarrassed.

There was a big, unspoken, "It wouldn't matter now," in the air.

Rachel felt a pang of sadness for her friend. At the same time she realized that unfortunately this little bit of information about Keith and another woman was sure to pique her mother's interest, if she decided to tell her.

"How did you meet Keith?" Becky asked, while stirring her diet cola with lemon.

"My father's friend, Becky Ralston, introduced us. He and Keith were acquaintances."

"From the country club?" Rachel said, remembering what her mother's friend Louise always said about the Ralstons.

Tori took a rather large sip of her wine and nodded. "That's for sure. I was raised with money, you might remember, but you would have thought the Ralstons spelled it with a capital M. You should see his wife, Gretchen."

"What do you mean?"

"The woman is a witch. She doesn't have a good thing to say about anyone. It's always, 'she's cheap, she's stupid, he drinks,' as if Bucky doesn't. She's even older than he is, but Bucky and Keith thought we could be friends, hang around the garden club, and play bridge."

"And?"

"I couldn't stand it. That's why we stopped seeing them."

"How did Keith know Bucky in the first place?"

As Tori answered, she looked at Rachel and Rachel knew the questioning was over. "I don't really know. Can we talk about something else?"

Rachel was more than happy to comply.

Tori was almost weepy when it came time to leave the girls and the restaurant. Although they'd exchanged telephone and cell numbers, as well as e-mail addresses, there was no guarantee that Tori would be able to reestablish her relationships with the other women. There seemed to be a hesitancy on their parts to understand Tori's feelings about Keith. She had chosen not to explain.

She was quiet for a moment after she started the car. "Some of you seemed to be unable to understand why I couldn't be with Keith. Really, though, it's quite simple. I couldn't trust him, and I don't mean with Alberta. I couldn't trust him with my feelings. Now do you understand?"

Rachel did not. For even though her own husband kept his feelings to himself, she knew he was always respectful of hers and would never do anything to hurt her. As much as she wanted to understand Tori, she needed more of an explanation.

Tears fell freely from Tori's eyes and they both sat for a minute in the cool of the car. "Do you want to tell me about it?" Rachel asked, taking out a tissue and handing it to Tori. She'd been brought up by her mother to always be prepared and today was no exception. "I won't betray your confidence."

Tori nodded. "He knew a secret about me. I don't

know if you know this, but I got into Yale. My parents were so proud, bragging to all their friends about how smart I was. But I wasn't. I never finished."

Rachel was surprised but she made sure not to let it show on her face. Tori, or Vicki, as she had been back when she and Rachel were friends, was always one of the smartest kids in school. She waited for Tori to go on.

Tori took a deep breath. "That wasn't the worst part. The reason I dropped out of college was because I got caught stealing the answers to a final exam for my boyfriend, who begged me to do it so he could pass his final and stay eligible for the basketball team. Then he pretended to know nothing about it and left me hanging. I was so humiliated at how stupid I was that I couldn't go back after the suspension they gave me. It was the biggest mistake of my life, until Keith, that is.

"He swore he'd never tell, but when he wanted the house, he threatened to tell everyone at the country club what I did. I could've faced that. I'm a lot more mature than I was in college, but I couldn't face what his threat meant—that he had so little regard for me that he would reveal my secrets if I didn't give him what he wanted."

"Do you think he really would have told someone?"

"I don't know. I've seen him do that before, with other people. If he ever knew anything about someone that the person didn't want known, Keith would use it or at least threaten to use it. He could be so mean. And that's why I couldn't stay with him."

Rachel understood. And she felt even sorrier for Tori.

* * *

"Look what I made, Mommy," said Gracie. She showed the decorated cardboard picture frame to her mother and allowed herself to be picked up for a hug.

Tori smiled at Wally. "How did you do this?"

Louise answered for her friend. "She practically has a whole crafts store in her basement, which all her friends help keep stocked with their discarded coffee cans and paper towel rolls. Children never leave this house without a finished product."

"Oh, pshaw," said Wally. "It isn't like that."

Louise winked at Tori. "Ask any kid in the neighborhood, or former kid. My house is full of projects from when my son and Debbie played together."

"I really appreciate everything," said Tori. "And I'm hoping we can keep in touch. You only live an hour away." She gave Rachel a hug, nearly upending the ungainly woman. "Don't forget to call the minute you have the baby."

Wally couldn't be sure, but she thought Tori might have had tears in her eyes as she left. The good-byes were lovely, but Wally could tell by Louise's face that her friend thought Tori was a bit needy. Louise had her opinions, and while Wally usually understood her views, she didn't necessarily agree with them. Besides, this woman was going through a stressful time—her child has lost her father and her house might still be at risk.

When Tori was gone Louise asked, "What did I do?"

Wally sighed. "I saw your face. You can be so judgmental."

"Said a person who is obviously being judgmental

about me," Louise pointed out. "What are you talking about anyway?"

Wally explained her thought processes just as Rachel came back into the kitchen after putting Jody down for a nap.

"I don't think she's wrong," said Rachel. "Tori is kind of needy, and in some ways she seems to be trying to convince people that she didn't know anything about Keith's business. At the same time she is explaining how she told him this was wrong and that it was a bad idea and whatever else."

"Did she get specific?" Wally asked.

"Tell us everything," Louise said, pulling up a chair.

The three of them sat at the kitchen table with two out of three sets of eyes glued on the pregnant woman. "Most of the time we were just talking about old times and that sort of thing. Tori and Nyla had a lengthy conversation about shoes, making me wonder which one of them is more likely to win the Imelda Marcos award."

Louise raised her hand. "I guarantee I am still the winner."

Wally nodded agreement.

Rachel chuckled before continuing. "When we were leaving, Tori told Amy, who opposes building in the quarry, she didn't agree with Keith when he bought the property. She said it was worthless."

"Obviously she didn't see the possibilities that Keith saw."

"That's just it. She says he never mentioned building in there. He just wanted to own it for some reason." The three women spent a while speculating on the meaning of that.

"Maybe he realized that just owning a hole in the ground, lush as it had become, was not enough," said Louise.

"I guess. But when he wanted to develop it and took on some partners, they required some cash up front from him. He didn't have any more, since he'd spent it all on the land in the first place, so he raided his daughters' college funds." Rachel's face showed she felt as disgusted by that as Wally did.

"Then he sold Tori's house," Wally reminded Louise. "At least he tried. Tell me, how did Tori act while she was telling you girls all of this?"

Rachel frowned. "She's a nice woman and I like her. I also feel sorry for her." She seemed reluctant to say more.

Louise patted her arm. "That's because you have a big heart. Now tell us how she acted."

"Oh, it was a mixture. She was sincere, I can tell you that, and sad, and, well, angry."

"Angry at Keith?" Wally asked. "Or at the person who killed him?"

Rachel looked up at her mother. "She never mentioned whoever killed him. She was mostly angry at Keith. I think it surprised the rest of the group. But they all seem to have better relationships with their husbands than Tori did. I don't think any of them can imagine being angry at someone for being murdered. But maybe it's just because they don't know the whole story."

"A lot of grieving people get angry at the person who dies," Louise said. "It's one of the stages of grief." Wally hoped she didn't notice the 'I know that, what do you think I was learning in college and graduate school?' look that Rachel gave her.

"This wasn't like that. It was more like she was angry at him for being so easy to hate."

Louise leaned forward. "Did she hate him? Enough to kill him?"

"No. At least I'm reasonably sure she didn't. Even though she thinks he cheated on her with Alberta Dellaquan and left her. She did say, and I believe her for reasons I won't share, that she could never love him again, and it wasn't because of the thing with the house or Alberta Dellaquan."

Louise opened her mouth to ask a question but the look on Rachel's face said don't bother.

Rachel turned to her mother. "Doesn't Tori have an alibi?"

Wally nodded. "At least I think so."

"Didn't either of you ever hear of murder for hire?" Louise asked.

Wally and Rachel stared at Louise. "That," said Wally, "is out of our investigative purview. I'll pass this information along to Dominique and let her figure out what to do."

Chapter Thirteen

Dominique answered her phone on the first ring and said she'd be right over. When she got there Wally told her about the conversation that Rachel and Tori had and hoped that Dominique would do whatever she needed to do.

As to the possibility of it having been murder for hire, Dominique told Wally that the police were fairly certain that Keith knew his assailant. "Keith wasn't dragged very far. Not many people would have stood close enough to a stranger at the edge of a cliff to be conked on the head and pushed into an abyss."

Wally felt a familiar jelly-kneed shiver as she imagined Keith at the cliff's edge and falling over. She shook it off as Dominique pulled out a piece of paper.

"This is a list of the people we think he had dealings with in the last several months," Dominique said, giving it to Wally. "We are in no way asking you to get involved in this, but is there anything you can tell me about these people?"

"How did you choose these people?"

"They're all people with whom Keith had some sort of negative contact. See what you think."

Wally took a look at the names. Along with Gabe Ferry and his wife Petra, whose property Keith fell from, were the three men he lived with, Norville Morgan, Randolph Quaker, and Dr. Izmir Fakhouri. Ron Walsh, the owner of the house, was also listed. Georgia Dewey was mentioned as a day care provider who lived nearby. Bucky Ralston's name appeared, since he was the man who sold the quarry to Keith and had tried to buy it back. Keith's business partners/golf buddies, Drs. Fuller, Ogden, and Armour, and his poker friends, Neal Dawson and Graham Fraser were all on the list, along with the other poker buddy, Boomer Revere, who had an ironclad alibi since he was out of the country. Keith's ex-wives Tori and Merle, and daughters Lara and Amber were also on the list. His secretary, sister, and a few other people also appeared. Dominique had put x's next to many of the names, leaving Ferry, Ralston, Graham Fraser, and the twins. She explained that each of the people crossed off the list had an alibi, eliminating him or her from suspicion.

"How could you think it was one of the girls?" Wally realized her voice had taken on a bit of an accusatory tone.

"We have an eyewitness who saw one of them driving up the hill at about nine-fifteen."

"Oh, sorry. Who?"

"A pizza delivery guy. He went to school with them but he doesn't know which one he saw, by the way."

"Few strangers can tell them apart. But what did they say?"

"They originally said they were together the whole time, but I think one went off with a young man and the other went for a drive. She ended up at a keg party."

"So which one do you suspect?"

"Lara."

Wally realized it wouldn't have mattered which of the twins was seen up near the top of the quarry. She didn't want either of them to be involved. It was too horrible to contemplate.

"As you know," Wally said, forcing herself to focus on Dominique's list, "I spoke to Georgia Dewey about what she saw at the house where Hollis was living. I'm not sure how accurate her assessments of her eyewitness accounts are, but I believe she saw what she said. As for the other people, I don't know the roommates, but I do know Ronny Walsh. He used to coach T-ball when Mark played. He's a nice man." She glanced at the list again. "Come to think of it, I also know Coach Morgan. Several of my friends' children were fencers in high school. I went to at least two meets to lend support." She paused trying to jog her memory.

It came back to her. "Georgia mentioned a fight between Coach Morgan and Keith. I wonder if it was about Amber. I think she's a fencer."

"I'll look into it," Dominique promised.

"And I know the Ralstons slightly," Wally said. "Gretchen and I were food bank co-chairs one year. Nate and I got to know both of them a bit better while we were trying to coordinate pick-ups, deliveries, and volunteers. They are nice people." She didn't add that she knew Tori Hollis did not share her opinion of Gretchen's good nature. It would only confuse the issue.

"Do you know anything about Mr. Ralston's relationship with Keith Hollis?"

"He introduced Tori to Keith. And Bucky sold him the property." She had an idea. "The quarry had been dormant for about fifteen years. Do you have any idea why Bucky suddenly chose to sell it?"

Dominique shook her head. "We're checking into Keith's finances. Maybe we should check into Ralston's finances as well."

That pleased Wally since it went along with Nate's follow-the-money idea, voiced after he heard what Rachel had learned. "It seems to me," she said, "that his father died several years ago. Maybe he didn't want his father to see the property sold, so he waited."

"It's possible. We'll see what we can find out. Thanks for the suggestion."

"What have you found out about Alberta Dellaquan of Dellaquan Builders?" Wally asked.

"Who?"

"Apparently Keith was having a relationship with her, both at the time of his first divorce and his breakup with Tori. Shouldn't we be looking into her story?"

Dominique's face said "What do you mean we?"

Aloud she said, "I'll look into that." She stood up to go. "But with your contacts and that knack you seem to have for people telling you their secrets, it would be great if you keep your eyes and ears open. We could use a break."

Wally nodded. She was already thinking of a few people she needed to visit. Now all she needed was a logical excuse for asking questions.

Rachel and Jody had gone to take Tillie, Nate's mother, to the town pool for the day. After a flurry of activity and gathering bathing suits, toys, books, and another box from the bakery full of Tillie's favorite coffee cake, Wally's daughter and granddaughter finally left. Nate had gone out much earlier. One of his friends had invited him to spend the day on his boat. Mark was in the Hamptons. Wally had the day to herself, as soon as she got home from day camp.

It was one of those July days that seemed to be a transplant from early May. The humidity was close to zero, or at least it seemed so, and the temperature was about 73. The sun was bright, but on the tree-lined streets of Grosvenor it remained cool.

She had promised to go to the pool with Louise later in the afternoon after the worst of the sun's damaging rays were gone, but Wally was restless. She had the afternoon to do whatever she wanted and she didn't have a clue what she wanted to do. It was too nice to read, even though she was reading a great book, and she realized what she needed was some exercise. If she got lucky, maybe she'd even spend some productive time thinking about the murder case. If not, at least she'd get a good workout. She could use it.

When she came back downstairs wearing her walking shoes, Wally saw her dog, Sammy, fast asleep on the floor with his feet up in the air, exactly the way he was when she went upstairs. "Wake up, you lazy boy," she said. "We're going for a walk."

She didn't have to ask twice. Sammy was instantly awake and waiting for his leash to be snapped on. "Just promise not to drag me," she begged the dog. Before they got the little black puppy with the big feet, she'd argued Labs were big and very strong, but she'd been overruled because of their good nature. And with the exception of an occasional unintentional run down the street, and several chewed things, Wally had never regretted adopting Sammy.

Sammy behaved himself and set off at a brisk but controllable pace. Wally directed him first to the park, which they crossed, and then beyond, not really with any particular goal in mind. She found herself walking past Ron Walsh's house, as well as Georgia Dewey's, and then into the section of town with large old houses and manicured lawns.

Many of the gardens showed evidence of the latest trend in Grosvenor. House after house, lately, or at least in Wally's opinion, had undergone extensive landscape makeovers including elaborate retaining walls. Everything, from the oldest shrubs to the tiniest weeds, had been removed and new plantings with lots of mulch had replaced them.

Wally had been working on her own garden for years and stopped to admire a few. Rows of impatiens, drifts of tiger lilies, as well as hanging baskets of petunias, ivy geraniums and wax begonias filled the streets with color, reminding Wally that New Jersey was the Garden State. The miles of oil refineries and other industry that people saw from the New Jersey Turnpike didn't typify the state.

On the next block Wally spotted a plant in a garden that she had been wanting for years but didn't know much about. To her surprise, she realized she knew the owner of the cadet-blue, center-hall colonial behind that garden. She decided to knock on the door and hoped that she could get the botanical information she wanted, and maybe something more. It could be her lucky day.

"We're stopping here," she told Sammy, whose tongue was hanging far out one side of his mouth. They could both use a drink, Wally realized, although that was too much to hope for. She'd settle for some information, and this might be the place to get it.

Gretchen Ralston opened the door almost immediately. "Wally," she exclaimed, "it is you. I was just coming in from the yard and I thought I saw you through the window. Why don't you come in?"

Wally was surprised by the warm greeting. Most people looked at Sammy as an unwelcome guest, even when they were guests in Wally's home. But Gretchen seemed to have an affinity for Sammy, which was explained as soon as they got through the front door. Her whole entryway was decorated in a black Labrador retriever motif.

"You're a beauty, aren't you?" Gretchen said to the dog. "Would you like a drink?"

Not sure whether she should respond since technically she hadn't been asked, Wally just made an *umhum* sound. The house was cool inside, even though the windows were all shut. The quiet swoosh of central air conditioning came from several vents unobtrusively dispersed around the walls.

Gretchen led them into the kitchen, placed a bowl of water on the floor for Sammy, and got Wally and herself a glass of pink lemonade. Wally was beginning to wonder why Gretchen was being so hospitable, after all, she had rudely dropped by unannounced. Even if Gretchen loved Labs, Wally's presence was still unexplained. She was about to open her mouth to give a reason for knocking on the door, when Gretchen burst out with, "I'm so glad you're here. I needed someone to talk to."

"Is something wrong?"

Gretchen looked at Wally and then away again. She seemed unable to decide where to start and instead apologized to Sammy for not having any treats. "I had two Labs of my own," she said. "You would have loved them."

Wally made some small talk about the dogs and waited for Gretchen to find the words she needed. It wasn't the first time someone had confided in her. People sometimes told her the most startling and personal things, although she had no idea why. Nate said it was because she could look so non-judgmental, particularly with strangers. The same was not necessarily true of friends and family, she knew. They could read her opinions like a newspaper.

One thing she knew about people taking her into their confidence was it often took a while to get started. Sammy tired of the whole thing and took a nap on the kitchen floor.

"The reason I'm here," Wally said, hoping that once explanations started flowing they would continue, and from both sides, "is because I've been wondering about that tall plant with the fuzzy white stems and the bright pink flowers. I think it looks so pretty the way you have it in the rock garden."

"Oh, thank you. It's lychnis."

As soon as she could, Wally planned to find out where to get the plant. For now she could just hope that Gretchen would get ready to spill her problems before Wally had to start walking home to meet Louise.

"Do you know who the police think killed Keith Hollis?" Gretchen said, her voice sounding strained. "It's been over two weeks already."

"No. Why do you ask?"

"You always know what's going on in town. And you solved those other cases, so the police would be crazy not to ask for your help."

Not wanting to take credit for anything, Wally stayed quiet.

Gretchen continued. "I wondered, um, have they eliminated any suspects?"

Wally did not divulge what she knew. "I couldn't say. Is there someone you are worried about?"

"Oh, no, of course not. It's just that maybe they might get the wrong idea."

"About what?"

Gretchen looked at Wally with worried eyes. "I gave them a statement, you know."

"You did? Why did they want to talk to you?"

"They were asking all the people who had dealings with Keith?"

"You had dealings with Keith?"

"No, not me. Bucky. He agreed to sell the quarry to Keith."

"Then why did they ask you?" Wally knew the answer, but she wanted to see what Gretchen thought about the questioning.

"They wanted me to corroborate what Bucky said. You know, his alibi." She practically whispered that word. Wally was willing to bet it was the first time Gretchen had even spoken to a police officer.

"What did you tell them?"

"That he was with me at the country club."

"He was?"

Gretchen's eyes fell. "Not exactly." She looked at Wally, as if hoping that Wally would give her some kind of dispensation once she'd confessed.

"What do you mean?"

"He was with me *most* of the time. All through the fireworks, and isn't that when they think Keith was killed?"

Wally bit her lip, wondering how she could explain it. "Yes, and no. They are fairly sure he was attacked during the town fireworks. The country club had theirs earlier."

"Oh."

"Where did Bucky go after that?"

"He went to smoke a cigar. There is a lounge for the smokers."

"Someone there should be able to verify that Bucky came in."

"I don't think so. Bucky told me that no one was there."

"Why does this worry you?"

"It didn't at the time. But now . . ." Tears formed in Gretchen's eyes. "I'm not sure he was there."

Wally didn't say a word. She had to let Gretchen compose herself.

"He was gone for so long. And when we left to go home, his car was in a different place."

"Could the valets have moved it?"

"Bucky doesn't use the valets. The parking lot isn't all that big anyway."

"Did you ask him about it?"

Gretchen chewed on her lower lip. "He said since there was no one in the smoking room he went for a drive to do it."

"For how long?"

She didn't answer.

"How long does it take to smoke a cigar?" Wally prompted, having no idea herself.

Still no response.

Wally was beginning to get the idea. "The car didn't smell like a cigar, did it?"

Gretchen shook her head.

"Are you worried that Bucky was involved?"

This time Gretchen nodded. "As much as I love him, if he did it, I wouldn't be able to deal with it."

Wally was getting really worried. But she was also getting nowhere, and she knew it. She had to learn something concrete. "Was there any bad blood between Bucky and Keith?"

"I really shouldn't be talking about this, but I'm worried. I'm sure it's nothing, but something happened."

"How so?"

"Bucky didn't want to go through with the sale soon after he agreed to it. He tried to cancel it but Keith threatened something called specific performance and said that if he didn't close he'd . . ." She took a deep breath. "Bucky has been trying to buy it back ever since Keith started talking about building, but Keith wouldn't budge."

"What did Keith threaten Bucky about?"

"I'm not sure I should be telling you this. Maybe we need a lawyer."

It was beginning to sound as if she was right, but Wally didn't want to stop her from talking. Whether any of this would shed light on the murder remained to be seen.

"It might be a good idea," Wally said.

Gretchen bit her lip for a moment. "There was something Bucky wanted and he went about getting it the wrong way. When he realized what he'd done he wanted to undo it. But he couldn't."

Wally gathered that selling the quarry had been Bucky's way of financing the thing he wanted, whatever it was, but she didn't know why that was a bad idea. "Why was selling the quarry wrong?"

"Because his father had wanted it to be given to the town to be used free for the public, in perpetuity."

"But it was Bucky's to decide what to do with it," Wally said. "His father had one opinion and Bucky, the heir, had his own. It was his right."

Gretchen gulped and blew her nose, all the while shaking her head. "No, it wasn't." Her voice was firmer now, and angry. "His father put it in a handwritten codicil and Bucky hid it."

"Wasn't there a witness?"

"Me."

"Didn't you tell him not to sell?"

"He never told me he was negotiating. It was too late when I found out."

"What did he need the money for?"

Gretchen looked at Wally, disbelief showing on her face. "He wanted to buy a minor league hockey team. I don't know what got into him. But his bid wasn't accepted, thank goodness. That's when he woke up and decided to do the right thing and pull out of the quarry sale."

Wally put her hand on Gretchen's. "Do you think that Bucky killed Keith?"

Her tears flowed freely. "I just don't know. I've lived with that man for 30 years, and I can't believe he's a murderer. He wasn't acting strange or guilty on that night, but he did lie to the police. Why would he do that?"

Wally could think of a few reasons, but none that

would make Gretchen feel better. "Have you tried talking to him? Maybe he has a good explanation and you are worrying for nothing."

"I tried, but he won't listen. Not about this, not about anything important. He just treats me like a princess, as if I'd break if I talked about finances or serious matters."

Wally was reminded that Gretchen had come from one of the finer old families, the ones with lots of money and breeding, who built great empires, people who were the ones the town was trying to erect a museum to honor. Bucky had come by his money through the quarry his father owned, and his family's roots were more blue collar.

The thought of the museum reminded Wally that she and Nate had promised to do what they could to find out who killed Keith Hollis before the July 31st museum contest deadline. The sooner they removed "unsolved murder" from the list of the town's attributes, the better.

Gretchen reached for Wally's arm. The movement caused Sammy to awaken and he went right back to wagging his tail happily at his hostess. She bent down and wrapped her arms around him, seeming to find strength. She looked up at Wally. "Maybe he'll listen to you. He has to come clean before the police find out he was lying."

"I'll do what I can," she promised, knowing it was about the last thing she'd want to do, but unable to think of a reason to suddenly keep her nose out of it. After extricating Sammy from Gretchen's grasp, she hotfooted it home.

"How was your visit with your grandmother?" she asked Rachel, who was dutifully drinking a glass of milk.

"Good. She's a pip. You should have seen the way she ran interference for me with the ladies in her building."

Wally had already had plenty of experience with the residents in Tillie's apartment building. They were more than a little outspoken. "Let me guess. They were all giving their opinions of what your baby will be." It was one of those things that Wally wondered about constantly, although she didn't voice it to Rachel. She almost wished Rachel had asked the doctor, but she and Adam had been firm in wanting their baby's gender to come as a surprise. All that matters, she told herself, is that it is a healthy baby. But a tiny part of her was really hoping for a boy.

"Exactly. One of them said she'd give me a girl on a silver platter."

Wally had heard that one when she was pregnant with Mark. "I wouldn't count on it."

Rachel giggled. "Another one wanted to hold a ring on a string over my stomach to see which way it would swing. Grandma said absolutely not and we made a run for it."

Way to go Tillie, Wally thought. But she couldn't help feeling a bit wistful that the truth hadn't come out.

She didn't have time to dwell on that, though. As Rachel went upstairs to rest, Wally ran out to meet Louise. She was energized and ready to do some serious laps.

Chapter Fourteen

After many attempts, Dominique and Ryan located Alberta Dellaquan at a job site. It turned out she was in the fencing business and she was busy supervising the installation of safety fencing at a house above the quarry.

"I'm sorry," said the woman who was in her early thirties. She wore construction boots, jeans, and a sleeveless work shirt that showed how much time she spent in the sun. "I honestly wasn't avoiding your calls. But we have been really busy up here and I have another ten houses waiting for us to get to work."

Dominique looked around. The house next door had a sign on its fence that proclaimed it was a Dellaquan installation. On the other side, workers wearing Dellaquan T-shirts were taking down an old rusty fence. "Business is good," Dominique noted. "You seem to have cornered the market."

While it was difficult to tell for sure if the tanned woman was blushing, her smile was that of someone pleased with herself. "We saw a potential opportunity and blanketed the neighborhood with signs and promotions."

"Is there someplace we can talk?" Dominique asked.

The smile slid off Alberta's face and she looked over at one of the workers. "I'm taking a break. Call me if you need anything."

"You are in charge of this job?" Ryan asked.

Alberta looked at him as if he were a Neanderthal, which, Dominique felt at that moment, was pretty much the truth. "I own the company," said the woman. "Lock, stock, and barrel."

That was a surprise to Dominique, although it explained at least partially why it was so hard to get to Alberta. "It's separate from Dellaquan Builders?"

There was a touch of defiance on Alberta's face. "Yes. I cut myself off from my family. Completely. And I built this from nothing. Now how can I help you?"

"We wanted to ask you about Keith Hollis," said Ryan, finally recovering from his earlier blunder. "We understand you had a relationship with the victim."

"That was a long time ago."

Ryan frowned then looked at his notes. "Are you saying you hadn't seen Mr. Hollis in the past few months?"

The move had the effect of stopping Alberta short. Dominique was reasonably sure Ryan didn't have anything written down about Alberta and Keith, since they had been unable to pin down any meetings, but Alberta couldn't know that. "I saw him. But we weren't . . ."

She stopped. "I know Tori thought I was back with Keith, but I wasn't. Not that way."

"When was the last time you saw him?" Ryan asked.

"Last month. Mid-June, I'd say."

"Where was that?"

"We had lunch in Union. At a diner. That's all. We were just friends. I understood what he was trying to build, but she didn't or she just didn't care to try. All she wanted was her beautiful house."

"Mrs. Hollis, you mean?" said Ryan.

"Who else?"

Dominique took over. "We'll need to know where you were on the evening of July fourth. And anything else you can tell us about Keith, including people who might have wanted to kill him."

"I was at Fire Island the entire weekend. With about fifteen housemates. And I could fill that whole notebook of his," she pointed at Ryan, "with people who hated Keith. Starting with my family."

"Was Mr. Hollis the reason for your split with your family?"

Alberta turned away and looked over the quarry. Hawks were flying around and landing on the upper reaches of the cliffs, giving Dominique the impression that they had nests there. Wild turkeys ran around down below. She allowed Ms. Dellaquan a moment to regroup, shooting Ryan a look to keep his impatience to himself.

When the woman turned back to the two detectives, Dominique could see that there were tears in her eyes. "Not entirely. He was the beginning of it, but not the whole reason." She angrily brushed away her tears. "It was just the tip of the iceberg. They took our relationship as a sign that I was a child and should be treated like one. Long after we'd broken up, my brothers would check up on the men I was dating. I got sick of it, and their attitude that I was someone they had to protect."

"You must have been quite young when you first knew Mr. Hollis," Dominique said. By her reckoning and from what she had heard, Alberta had been about sixteen and working for the family business on Saturdays to make some spending money. Keith had just dropped out of college after two years to go work for the Dellaquans and had been accepted by the family as one of them. He was moving up in the business and learning all aspects of it until the head of the family found out about Keith's dalliance with his daughter. It cost him not only his marriage, but also his job.

"I was young and stupid," said Alberta. "But I grew up. They just couldn't see that and they wouldn't let me do anything important in the business. So a couple of years ago I decided I'd had enough of them and I started my own business. It's taken me a while, but I'm doing better every day."

Dominique could sympathize with her. She'd also had people in her life who just couldn't or wouldn't take her seriously. It only made her want to prove herself more. But starting a business wasn't the easiest thing in the world. "Just like that?" Dominique the woman.

Defiant anger crossed Ms. Dellaquan's face. "Yes. I got a loan."

Dominique would look into that. It seemed impossible that a young woman could get a loan like that by herself. Perhaps her friendship with Keith Hollis included his co-signing that note. It was worth checking out. "It sounds like that business with your family was a long time ago. Do you know anyone else who might have wanted to hurt Mr. Hollis? Other than your family, I mean."

The woman looked at the ground. "I never met his family or any of his friends. I wouldn't know anything about it."

Dominique handed her a business card and asked her to call if she thought of anything else. There didn't seem to be a connection to the murder, but she would make sure every bit of Ms. Dellaquan's story was true.

Rachel came into the kitchen just as Wally was finishing the dinner dishes. Jody, squeaky clean from her bath, and obviously sleepy, trailed behind her. "We're ready, Mom."

Wally was pleased that Rachel had kept Jody up until sundown, which was so late in the summer, for the lighting of the Shabbat candles. She dried her hands and took out a box of matches from the drawer. She already had the Shabbat candles ready, in their enameled holder with the image of a woman covering her face in between the two candles. It had been a gift from Rachel on the occasion of her bat mitzvah, and Wally had used it ever since. It had more meaning than Rachel could know—Wally had never seen her own mother, Judith, light the Shabbat candles, although she had seen her grandmother do it. That had led to a weekly reminder of her loss, after her grandmother died and her mother did not take up the practice. Wally, at eleven, had taken to lighting the candles herself. If the taking over of the mother's role in lighting the candles had affected her mother in any way, Wally never knew. Oddly, Judith always made a big deal of watching Wally do it when the grandchildren were small. Then again, a lot of things had been different with the new generation.

Jody, Judith's namesake, beamed with pleasure when Wally lit the match. Unprompted, the child chanted the prayer for lighting the candles, nearly perfectly. Rachel looked at Wally with a mixture of pride and emotion in her eyes. Wally swallowed hard and smiled back.

The next morning, at synagogue, Jody sang along with the closing songs of the Sabbath service. After the Kiddush was sung and the challah and wine distributed, several people came over to say hello to the Morris family.

"She's beautiful," said the cantor, whose richly melodious voice had uplifted everyone at the service. He looked at Rachel as if in surprise. "I can't believe that I bat mitzvahed you only a few years ago, and you already have a daughter and another baby on the way."

Rachel smiled. "I won't mention how long ago that was if you won't."

The cantor seemed to accept that as a good idea. After he went to greet another family, one of the older women in the congregation came to see Wally and Nate and their family. She was fussily dressed as always,

Wally noted, as she braced herself. "Voltairine," said the woman, whose name was Gilda, "how are you?" Gilda always called Wally by her legal name for some reason, not caring that Wally disliked it and never used it unless she was doing something that required it, such as voting or testifying in court, when use of a legal name was mandatory.

Without waiting for a response, Gilda turned to Rachel, who was holding Jody, and started chirping at the little girl. "Aren't you gorgeous?" she cooed. "The prettiest girl here."

Rachel thanked Gilda on behalf of her daughter, but the woman was already onto her next subject. "Are you going to find out who killed that nice Keith Hollis?" she asked Wally. "He came to talk to us at one of our senior center meetings and he was just so wonderful. We would have saved so much in taxes if he had built what he wanted in the quarry."

Nate had a puzzled look on his face. It matched the sincere doubts Wally felt about the savings the seniors would have realized if the building project had gone forward as planned. She began to wonder what other exaggerations Keith had made, and whether one of them was responsible for his death. All Wally could do now, though, was make sad clucking noises and move on.

Chapter Fifteen

Wally pulled into the driveway at Merle Hollis's house and got out of the car. She had called earlier to say she was bringing over something for the family and hoped they would all be home.

Merle answered the door and invited her in, gratefully taking the lemon chiffon cake that Wally had made the night before. She couldn't go there empty-handed and she had needed to come. She had to help get Lara Hollis's name off the suspect list. Dominique's promise that it was nothing to worry about hadn't reassured Wally enough to let the police handle it. Certainly not now, days after that promise was made.

"You are so kind to bring this," Merle said. "Can I offer you something cold to drink?"

"No thanks. I just wanted to see how you were doing. How are the girls?"

"You know," said Merle. "It's odd. They were always

185

such daddy's girls, or at least tried to be. Keith may not have noticed, but they adored him. And to a certain extent, I think they held themselves back from becoming adults. But now—" She broke off, hearing footsteps on the stairs.

Two young women came into the living room where Wally and Merle sat. They looked different, though, from the girls who attended their father's funeral just a few weeks earlier. Each had her long hair trimmed and styled, differently, Wally noted, and one no longer had brown hair; it was now a deep red.

"You look wonderful," Wally exclaimed. "All ready for college."

"They are," said Merle. "We managed to get the finances cleared up so they will both be going to the schools of their choice." She looked greatly relieved.

Wally wasn't so relieved. It almost seemed as if Keith's death had been a good thing. And the nagging thought that Lara, who Wally was pretty sure was now the red head, might have had something to do with it, dug into her sense of well-being. Wally had more questions to ask, but she was still smarting from the last time she asked Merle questions. She struggled to find the words.

Merle waited expectantly. Wally wished she had opted to take the drink, because then she'd have had a reason to linger.

"I know this is still a hard time for you," Wally said, treading carefully. She looked over at the twins. "And I've been in contact with the police, so I know they haven't figured out yet who killed your father."

"Is there something you want to know?" asked Merle.

"Believe me, I am only trying to help. I know that no one in this house had anything to do with it, but we have to make sure the police understand that."

"It's me, isn't it?" Lara said. "They don't believe me because I can't account for every minute between the time I left the park and when I arrived at the party at ten. But I didn't even see my father that night."

"Why did you leave before the fireworks were over?" Wally asked.

"Amber's boyfriend was doing that three's a crowd thing. I decided to see if I could see the fireworks from up the hill."

Shivers ran down Wally's spine. Had Lara been near the scene of the crime that night? She was practically holding her breath when she asked, "Where did you go?"

"I pulled into the garage of that big apartment house on the hill. Then I went up the stairs to the roof. I got a really good view of not only our fireworks, but all the surrounding towns. It was awesome."

Merle looked surprised. "That was private property."

"I didn't do anything to it. I just stood there. And I stayed after the fireworks were over, just looking at the New York skyline, at my future. It was so beautiful."

"She's going to NYU," Merle explained, although Wally had been aware of that.

"I don't suppose you saw anyone who could vouch for your story," Wally asked.

"There was a cat, although I doubt he'd vouch for me. He just sat there, even though his owner kept calling for him, the whole time I was there. The owner finally came into the garage and the cat went over to him. They left and I left right afterward."

"Did the owner see you?" Amber asked, looking hopeful.

"No."

The three of them looked defeated. But Wally still held out hope. "Do you remember the name of the cat?"

"Gimlet."

"Maybe that will help."

"How?"

"If his owner was looking for him as you say, maybe his owner will provide an alibi."

"How are you going to find the owner?"

"I have sources," Wally said cryptically. Merle's face told her she knew who they were, and, at least this time, didn't mind at all.

Wally arrived home just in time to see Omega run into her backyard. She opened her back door and asked the dog if he wanted to go for a ride. The question had the desired effect and Omega jumped right in.

It didn't take long to drive up the winding hill to Gabe's and Petra's house. "Your mommy is going to be happy to see you," Wally said. Omega seemed quite content to be in the car, after settling in to the exact spot where Sammy always sat. Once he saw all the police cars and people in front of his house, he whined to be let out.

Gabe came out of the house when Wally pulled into the driveway. He seemed happy to see his dog but his face was pale. "They think I did it," he said. "They are tearing everything apart." He looked at Omega. "They made me put him outside even though the fences are still down. It was only supposed to be for a minute and then I could put him back in the basement, but he bolted right away. Petra is out looking for him."

"You should tell her he's back," Wally said, realizing that Gabe was close to a nervous breakdown. He nodded, pulled out his cell phone, and made the call.

"Why did the police come back?" Wally asked, wondering where Dominique was and how soon she could talk to her.

Gabe sat down on his back steps. "They said my story didn't check out."

Wally sat next to him. "What do you mean? You were at the fireworks like everyone else, weren't you?"

"Yes and no. I was where I always am on July fourth watching the fireworks. But it was on the Nortons' deck."

"So then you had witnesses." Wally couldn't see the problem at all.

"Again, yes and no. I left right afterwards to let Omega out of his crate in the basement. I always lock him up while there are fireworks because they make him crazy."

"But you were there during the actual fireworks, right?"

"Yes. All of them. I really love to watch them."

Wally was perplexed. "I can't see what the problem is."

"No one remembers seeing me during the actual show and for a short time thereafter. But I was here right after the fireworks, letting Omega outside for a minute before going back."

Wally turned to him in surprise. "Omega was out in the yard after the murder?"

Gabe stared back at her. "I guess he was."

"If only he could talk," Wally said. "Tell me. Did he act like anything was strange?"

"He's been acting strange since the construction started. Every time he went out after the workmen had been here he'd sniff every single footstep."

"Sammy does that too," Wally admitted, chuckling, hoping to break the tension. "After the gardener has been there, especially. And based on his frantic running around in the morning, there are a lot more deer coming through our yard than I thought."

Gabe nodded, finally looking a bit less pale. "I'll tell you this, though, he ran around exploring near the edge a lot more than usual. My heart was in my mouth worrying that he'd fall over and I hurried him along and into the house."

Wally, who had been listening intently, wondering if it was significant, felt the familiar shiver she got at the thought of high precipices. She'd been avoiding looking at the edge of Gabe's property since she drove in but it didn't work. "Why aren't the fences up yet?" she asked, trying quell her imagination. "How long does it take?"

"We've been put on hold. The contractor had to move on while the police had the property cordoned off." He gestured at the yellow tapes strung from sticks placed around the perimeter. "We may have to wait weeks to finally get the fence."

Wally watched a moment as the leaves on the trees

just below the edge suddenly blew in the breeze. It was a relatively calm day and she turned to Gabe in puzzlement.

"Updrafts," he said, by way of explanation. "They're quite strong sometimes. The red-tailed hawks seem to have fun flying on them."

Wally wanted to stop the discussion of things that were flying over the edge of the cliff. "What did you do after you brought Omega back into the house?"

"I went back to the party right away," Gabe said, "since I knew he would be fine."

She knew it was ridiculous, but Wally trusted Gabe and not just because he was a good dog parent. He had been a scout leader for as long as Mark was a scout, and although Mark wasn't in his troop, Wally felt people in scouting were fine and upstanding. Nate would agree, she was sure. But she could see the police's point of view. At the very least, Gabe may have had opportunity, since the timing of the attack on Keith was somewhat uncertain. Yes, according to Dominique they knew when Keith attempted to make a call and didn't finish it, but there was nothing to say that he hadn't changed his mind and hung up. If that were the case, the murder could have occurred after the fireworks.

"Can you think of any possible motive the police think you might have had?" Wally knew it was a dopey question to ask a murderer, but she was sure she was not talking to one.

"People would say that I was his most outspoken opponent against the building in the quarry. But I realized it wasn't a problem, so there goes the motive, if that were even one." He looked at her. "I could never kill a person, at least not over something like that."

Wally decided not to wonder what circumstances might lead Gabe to murder. He probably, she reasoned, did not mean that the way it sounded. "Why wasn't it a problem?"

"There's no way he can ever build there. The water table is too high. There is no place for storm water to go. I would have thought it was obvious that if you dig a hole it will fill with water, but I guess not. That's why I had an independent hydrogeologist evaluate the property. He said the site makes it impossible to redirect storm water runoff."

"But couldn't Keith have found someone else who could have designed an adequate storm water runoff plan?"

Gabe paled again, as pale as he had been before. "I didn't think of that. I mean, my guy has the best credentials. But if he did that, then I guess . . ."

Wally realized that in some ways she was dealing with a babe in the woods. And this babe was in a lot of trouble. She looked forward to talking to Dominique.

Wally was getting ready to leave the nursery school at the end of an uncomfortably hot day, when one of the fathers came inside to pick up his child. Wally asked him to wait while the car pool line was in progress. When she came back to tell him he could pull his car out, she found him grilling his child with questions about the letters and numbers hung on the walls and he didn't seem ready to leave.

He pointed to some more pictures. "What's this letter?" A second later it was "How many monkeys are in that picture?"

The child was small, one of the early threes who was in Renee's class. He had about a seventy-five percent correct response rate, which was good for his age, but his father kept pushing him, when he was wrong, to try again. The child became more and more frustrated, until he finally started to cry.

Wally wondered how the father would have felt if someone constantly badgered him to be perfect, the way he badgered his little boy.

By the time they had pulled out of the parking lot ahead of her, Wally was as frustrated as that little boy. Having no leads on the case, which looked as if it were going to land someone she respected in jail, someone she was sure didn't commit the crime, didn't make her feel any better.

Her recent conversation with Dominique hadn't helped. All it did was raise more questions. For one, why did Keith's former secretary leave? Wally didn't feel she could ask Tori, but maybe Rachel could. Adam was still away and she had decided to stay in town a few more days, but she hadn't called Tori as far as Wally knew. Another thing that bothered her was Kelley Perren, and Wally decided she would have to talk to her. She also wished she could get to know those golf buddies of Keith's, especially since they were investors, and she began to wonder which investor Peggy meant when she said one was pulling out. She also thought she should confront Bucky, on the theory that he'd probably prefer to explain himself to her rather than the police.

Wally realized she was still driving behind the overly demanding father and his son. The thought of having to be perfect resurfaced again and with it Peggy's comment about people unrealistically expecting Keith to be perfect when he came to live with her. Louise had not told her the specific nature of the things that Keith had done back in school that required Peggy to seek the assistance of an attorney. Maybe Dominique could help.

"Assault, burglary, truancy, and possession," said Dominique when she returned Wally's call later in the afternoon. Wally and Jody were playing a card matching game while Rachel took a long-needed nap. She had driven up to Westchester for a doctor's appointment and come straight back down, exhausted.

"That's good," Wally told Jody, since the child had just finished grouping her cards.

The voice on the other end of the phone said, "I beg your pardon?"

"Oh, sorry, Dominique. I was playing with my granddaughter. Are you saying that Keith was some kind of delinquent?"

"What's delinquent?" Jody asked, perfectly mimicking the new word she had overheard.

Imagining Rachel's face when she heard about it, and her caution to always watch what she said in Jody's presence, Wally said, "Oy." It wasn't as if, as a nursery school teacher for all those years, she didn't already know that. "A bad person."

Jody seemed satisfied with that for the present and went back to her version of shuffling the cards, which was to mix them around until they fell off the table and had to be picked up. Wally turned her attention back to the phone.

"What did he do?"

"Keep in mind that the records are all sealed, since he was a minor at the time. I had to get this information from old neighbors of Keith and Peggy's, and they might not have the whole story straight. Most notable, according to at least two different people, was his fighting. He was big and strong. And he traveled with three other boys, also football players. Sometimes they tried to clean up the parks."

"I sense you are speaking in euphemisms."

"Quite right," said Dominique. "According to what I heard, he and his friends had, on occasion, attacked groups of boys from out of town whom they felt should not be hanging around in Grosvenor's parks."

"The parks are open to the public," Wally pointed out, unnecessarily, she knew. "Who put them in charge?"

"I guess they put themselves in charge. As soon as the police heard about it, they broke up the fights."

"Gangs?"

"Not back then. No. Just insider versus outsider."

"How long did that go on?"

"That's not clear, but Keith's days doing it were ended by his kidney donation. The neighbors were impressed by his altruism and believed it probably changed his life for the better. He couldn't risk fighting anymore. And according to his school counselor he really changed in his senior year, studied more, and focused on his band and trying to get into college without relying on football. He was never implicated in anything after that."

"Were some of the names of the other boys Dawson and Fraser?"

"No. I asked the counselor about them. They became friends after Keith turned over his new leaf. He stopped hanging out with the other boys a few months after the surgery."

"Did the other boys continue their . . ."—she searched for a word—"bad behavior?" Jody gave her a quizzical look.

"As I said, it isn't clear, but it seems unlikely, since Keith was basically the ringleader."

"And he had been an outsider himself," Wally said, thoughtfully. "Do we think any of the other boys might have been involved with Keith recently?"

"I checked. One of the neighbors knew two of the boys' names. We know that two of the boys are dead— one in Desert Storm and one the first week of college, when he wrapped himself around a tree. I'm going to check for other connections. Thanks for the idea."

Wally shivered. So much tragedy. "I hope it helps," said Wally. After hanging up, she put all thoughts of the investigation out of her mind and concentrated on Jody, who had moved on to a new game. Life was too precious and times like this were not to be wasted.

Chapter Sixteen

Captain Jaeger wanted another update. It was the third one this week, and there was nothing new to report. Because of the problems with contamination at the scene of the crime there were no usable forensic leads, with the exception of the jacket fiber found on the shovel shaft. Davis was convinced that Gabe Ferry was their man and had been able to convince a judge to issue a warrant. Dominique and Ryan had been part of a team that spent several hours searching Ferry's house and going through his office records. Nothing had turned up that would implicate him or even tie him to Keith Hollis, except their both being candidates in the upcoming local election. Even then, the campaign literature that Ferry had in mockups did not mention anything about the proposed building in the quarry. Dominique felt that gave more strength to Wally Morris's conviction that Gabe Ferry had nothing to do with Keith's death.

The focus on Professor Ferry detracted from the possibility of investigating other potential suspects. But as usual, Jaeger was backing the winning horse, or at least the strong suspect in the county's view, and did not give permission to Dominique or Ryan to look elsewhere.

Throughout the meeting Jaeger maintained the same calm he had been displaying since the department meeting on interpersonal relationships, but that wasn't always the case. He ran hot and cold in his ability to sustain a civil attitude in the face of pressure to conclude the case. Dominique hoped he would maintain his calm, even if their chief suspect was eliminated.

The Grosvenor town council meeting took several extra minutes to come to order, since this was the first time this body, for which Keith Hollis had been a candidate, was meeting since his murder. The news media had sent out news crews, it being another slow news day, and the cameramen filled the balcony above the meeting room, taping the proceedings.

Once the room had quieted, the village clerk read a statement concerning Mr. Hollis, expressing sympathy, and then normal business resumed. The biggest problem, though, was the standing motions tabled at the last meeting pending engineering surveys. No one seemed to know whether the development plans died with Keith Hollis. The meeting stumbled along, interrupted by the ringing of cell phones, one of which belonged to a council member who loudly told her child he could not stay up for another half hour.

Twenty minutes were spent reporting on and discussing the latest steps being taken in the effort to convince Dolores Hampton that the museum of nineteenth century history should be built in Grosvenor. The town parks and recreation officer read a list of citations he had issued for excessive grass height and trees and shrubs blocking sidewalks. He was proud to announce full compliance in repairs by the cited residents.

Wally and Nate had chosen to sit in the back of the room to give support to Gabe Ferry who, even though he knew he was a prime suspect in Keith Hollis's murder, felt he should make his usual council meeting appearance since he had nothing to hide. On the way into the meeting chamber, at least a half dozen people had told Nate that he should now run for council in Keith's place.

Nate just shook his head for the first five comments. "But you are against the building in the quarry and you can ensure that it doesn't happen," the people argued.

"I wouldn't want to be a one-issue candidate," Nate said, by way of answer to the last person who asked. "And we really don't know what is going to happen." Wally knew that Nate knew his candidacy was ridiculous, not because he wouldn't have been a great council member, because he would have, but because the deadline for filing a candidacy petition, at least this year, was long past.

"I can't understand why people think I should run," he said, when they were home.

Wally turned on the news to see if her town would be shown. "Face it, Nate, you've lived in this town for almost thirty years and have always expressed your opinions on how things are run. And you would be good."

"Look," he said. "There's B. J. Waters standing in front of town hall."

"No one is there anymore," Wally pointed out. "Everyone went home."

Nate edged closer to the television. "I guess they think it makes it seem more legitimate if the reporter is on location. At least they aren't in front of poor Tori's house with their Klieg lights this time."

"Hmph." Wally could not say more because B. J. was speaking.

"Trouble broke out tonight in the small town of Grosvenor, New Jersey where residents are still reeling from the July fourth murder almost three weeks ago of a town council candidate. Police have not made an arrest yet but suspects include a rival candidate."

"What trouble?" Nate whispered, "I didn't see any trouble."

They soon saw what the reporter meant. Several seconds of footage of the meeting before it was called to order did make it look as if there was some sort of problem. The arrival of several officers and the subsequent quieting of the crowd had only been coincidental. The officers had come because they were being thanked for their efforts on the July Fourth celebration and only the curiosity of the crowd had made them quiet down to listen to what was being said.

The voiceover repeated the same thing that B. J. had said when she was "live," adding no clarification whatsoever. The only conclusion that Wally could draw was that the report was an attempt by the station to bring up the murder and appear to be on top of the investigation.

"Back to you," B.J. said. The eleven o'clock anchor shook his head. "It must be difficult for the residents of the town at a time like this."

His co-anchor agreed. "Very difficult." She paused and shook her head. "Another town with a headache in our area is . . ." Nate had turned off the TV so Wally never got to find out what town that might be. Still, they had her sympathy.

"Thanks for seeing me," Wally said, as she took her seat in Bucky Ralston's office.

"I'm going to be honest with you," Bucky said. "I did not want to meet with you. But Gretchen asked me to."

Wally was not in the mood for another hostile person. This morning at the nursery school had been enough, with Van, the contractor, loudly disagreeing with Abby on her first day back after breaking her leg. She was having a difficult time getting around and not at all satisfied with the handicap access that Van's crew had installed.

"It's up to code," Van had insisted.

"Then why do I feel as if I'm about to fall? This ramp is so slippery that a wheelchair would slide back down."

"That's because it isn't finished. You don't belong in the construction zone."

Things had settled down by the time the children arrived. But Van was still grousing to Wally about it afterwards. "Is something else bothering you?" she asked. "Is there anything I can do?"

"Your boss is so impatient. If it wasn't for this lousy economy I'd be outta here in a heartbeat. Those guys in Washington don't care about us little people."

Wally wasn't interested in hearing a diatribe about the government at the moment. She turned to go but Van reached out, putting his hand on her arm. She turned back.

"I'm sorry," the contractor said. "It's very nice that you are concerned about me. Yes, there is a problem."

Waiting, Wally said nothing.

"It's the economy. There aren't any jobs coming in. And the one I had, small as it was, cancelled. If the people who ran this country had their heads on straight, this wouldn't be happening."

Wally wanted to avoid the political discussion. "A job cancelled?" she said.

The red that was suffusing Van's face began to disappear as he nodded sadly. "Yes. Just yesterday. And I was getting all ready to place her order, since we'll be done with this job soon."

That was good news, and Wally wanted to hear more about it. But Van was still stuck with his misery. "That woman!"

"Abby?"

"Her, too. No, I meant that Peren woman. She had me over there every week with new ideas of what we were gonna do. Then she cancelled. Not enough money for the job, she said. I tell you, this country is going down the toilet."

Wally's ears had perked up when he said the customer's name. "You were going to do some work for Kelley Peren?"

"Yes, she wanted us to do a bathroom. I was going to do it myself, off the books, so I could keep a little more of what our government likes to steal from me. The job didn't need a whole construction crew. But now I don't even have that."

"You'll get something else," Wally said, still puzzling over why Kelley's name would come up. Something had her wondering about Kelley's connection, if any, to Keith's ending up in the bottom of the quarry, the same quarry which Kelley repeatedly told the readers of the local paper was dangerous.

It was getting late. "I really have to run," Wally said. "I hope you get some big contracts soon."

She had made it with only seconds to spare to Bucky's office in the Jersey City economic development zone where he had recently relocated the small manufacturing company his father had purchased when he closed the quarry. Bucky gave her a brief tour of the factory, showing her several of the tiny metal widgets, or whatever he called them, that his company made. "Ninety percent," he'd said, proudly. "Ninety percent of all the ones made in this country are made right here. If those big car manufacturers need one of these, they come to me. If they need it made a little differently, I'm the man to modify it." He chuckled. "Or at least my engineers are." But his mood changed when they went into his office and she mentioned why she was there.

"Gretchen is worried about you," Wally told him. He stiffened and gritted his teeth, looking as if he would never open his mouth again, let alone have a conversation with Wally about the problem. For several awkward moments she was sitting with him, his silence, and his hostility.

He took a pack of antacid tablets out of his shirt pocket and separated one, leaving the empty wrapper on his desk. After he had chewed it up he said, "Gretchen should get a hobby. I'm fine. There is nothing to worry about."

Wally didn't say anything. But she didn't get up to leave either, and eventually Bucky looked up. "What is she so worried about anyway?"

"She thinks there is some time on the evening of the murder that is unaccounted for. Some time when you weren't where you said you were."

Bucky folded the antacid wrapper into a tiny square before he spoke. "I was having a cigar."

"I know that's what you told the police, but your wife doesn't think so. She isn't doing this to hurt you. She is really worried. The police will find out you were lying, you know."

"I went for a drive. To clear my head."

"In the middle of the July Fourth celebration?"

Bucky looked at Wally for a long time, as if assessing her for her discretion. She must have passed because he let out a long sigh and leaned forward. "I was rehearsing. I wanted to talk to Keith, to convince him to let me buy back the quarry. I was practicing my arguments, rebutting his, at least what I thought he'd say, and trying to figure out what to do if he turned me down."

"Why did you want it back so badly?"

"I realized I should never have sold it."

"Gretchen said you were trying to buy a minor league hockey team, but the bid wasn't accepted. Didn't you want to try for another team?"

"No," Bucky said. "It was all a crazy idea. A mistake. I don't even know what made me want to do it."

Wally didn't offer a possible explanation. She certainly didn't mention Nate's theory, that Bucky wanted to join his country club friends and manufacturing cohorts in owning flashy things such as sports teams, race horses, and small islands. There was a lot of money in Grosvenor and even more in some of the surrounding towns and some of the people with it liked to show off. Until Bucky's father passed away, Bucky and Gretchen had always lived just an upper middle-class lifestyle. His father had not exactly shared his wealth, other than sending Bucky to all the right schools. The Ralstons' fancy house had come from Gretchen's family. Her old money had met his new money in school and they had fallen in love. But he had never impressed anyone else in her family and that family had not had much to do with them. Now that he had inherited his father's quarry money and was having so much success with growing his company, Bucky was moving in fancier circles, with the country club set. And if Nate was right, Bucky was learning to show off.

"What I should have done," Bucky continued, "is what my father wanted. I should have given the quarry to the town, for a park." He didn't mention that it was a part of his father's will that he hadn't been forthright about, and Wally didn't tell him that Gretchen had shared this information with her.

"That would have been wonderful," was all she said.

"I'm going to try to buy the quarry back from Keith's estate and do right by my father." He paused. "Oh, does that make it sound like I had a motive to kill him?"

Wally wondered if that might be true. "Can you be more specific about where you went on July fourth? Did anyone see you? You might need a witness."

"I didn't drive anywhere near the quarry, if that's what you mean. I drove out Route 78 to 287 then up to 24 and back to the country club. I have a Porsche. I wanted to be able to open it up on the road. I can't do that on the steep winding hills around Grosvenor."

It certainly sounded plausible to Wally, that, or carefully rehearsed. And she couldn't see any way to prove it even if it was the truth. "None of those roads were toll roads," she said, "so there wouldn't be an E-Z pass record. I don't suppose you stopped for gas or anything?"

"Why are you asking me these questions?"

"To see if you have an alibi."

Bucky stared at her.

"What's wrong?"

"I'm wondering how your mind works."

"Logically. If you don't have an alibi, someone may think you killed Keith."

White-faced, Bucky shook his head. "I don't have one. But I didn't do it."

"You'd better tell the police what you've told me," Wally said. "Someone may have seen you leave or return to the parking lot, and without anyone knowing where you went, one could conclude that you did go to the quarry."

Bucky pulled out the stomach tablets again and took another one. "I don't know how I'd prove it," he said, folding the wrapper into another tiny square. "They'll just have to take my word for it."

"I think the first person you'll need to convince is your wife," Wally said, standing and ready to leave. "She really cares what happens to you."

The previous unconcerned nothing-I-can-do-about-it-if-she-doesn't-trust-me look vanished. "I'll convince her," Bucky said soberly. "She is the only one I have to answer to."

Wally wondered if that was true as she drove away. She still felt unsettled about her conversation with Bucky when she got home. As she picked up the local paper on her way into the house, it reminded her of her earlier conversation about Kelley Peren. Wally wondered if there would be yet another letter to the editor about the quarry, and then she wondered why Kelley had suddenly found herself unable to afford the renovations she had wanted. It didn't seem likely that there would be a connection between the two situations.

Rachel had just come back from a walk with Jody and said that the two of them were going upstairs to take a rest. Wally decided to use the time wisely. "I'll be back before you wake up," she promised.

Wally used the phone book she kept on the back seat of her car to look up Kelley Peren's address. But for a moment she felt she must have had it wrong. Kelley didn't live anywhere near the quarry, so why would her cat have been in a tree at the edge? Even if her cat had walked so far from home, how would Kelley have known to go there to look? Something was fishy and it wasn't the cat food.

Kelley's house was the second one in from the corner on the same street as one of the town's elementary schools. Pink and white impatiens lined the path up to the house and there were flowerpots on each stair step. Wally went up onto the porch and rang the door bell.

"Yes? Can I help you?" asked the young woman who opened the door. She looked a little older than Rachel.

Wally realized she might be biased in her assessment and that she might just look more sophisticated, no offense to Rachel. Kelley had a short hair style that framed her face and wore long artsy earrings that were, in Wally's opinion, anything but understated.

She introduced herself and explained that she was looking into the circumstances surrounding Keith Hollis's death. "I hope you can help me," she added.

Without even opening the screen door, Kelley asked, "What makes you think I can?"

It was awkward standing there like that, but Wally persevered. "I understand you wrote several letters to the local newspaper about the danger at the quarry."

"I almost fell in," Kelley said, somewhat defensively. "My poor cat was almost scared to death."

At that moment a cat, seemingly without any leftover effect of the experience at the quarry, walked onto the porch and stood expectantly in front of the door. Kelley pushed it open and, as somewhat of an afterthought, invited Wally inside.

"I can only stay a minute and I'm not trying to make

any trouble," Wally assured her. "I'm just trying to understand something."

Kelley blinked. "What?"

"Your letters to the editor. You wrote so many. Did you have another scare at the quarry after the time you tried to rescue your cat?"

"No."

"Did you hear of someone else who had a bad episode?"

"No."

Wally decided to try another question, one that would require more than a mono-syllabic answer. "How did your cat get up to the quarry in the first place?"

Kelley paled and looked over at her cat. "It wasn't Petunia. It wasn't even really my cat. I was in the school yard overlooking the quarry, taking pictures, since the bare trees let me get a better view of everything. It's really beautiful up there, you know. Then I heard a cat meowing and found it in a tree. I just couldn't leave it there."

"Whose cat was it?"

"I don't know. It doesn't really matter, does it? I made it seem like it was my cat, since it sounded better. It was really stupid. Keith Hollis called me after he read about my experience in the paper and came up with the idea. I felt funny about doing it, but it was true, it could be dangerous."

"If there weren't any more incidents, why did you keep writing the letters?"

"Because I was worried that sooner or later someone would fall into the quarry. And you see, someone did."

"Do you mean Keith?"

"Yes."

"But he fell in before your last letter appeared. And you didn't even mention it."

Kelley looked to be at a loss for words. Wally gave her time to think of an answer and took a minute to look around the house. It was adorable on the inside, arts and crafts-style decorations were everywhere, and there were beautiful textile throws on the twin love seats. "I didn't find out that he died until yesterday."

Little alarms went off in Wally's head at hearing the coincidence of Kelley's cancellation of the renovation the same day she found out about Keith's death. There had to be a connection.

While it was strange that Kelley hadn't heard about the biggest event in town in recent memory, Wally wondered if there was some significance to her learning of the murder yesterday. "How did you find out?"

Kelley bit her lip. "You'll think I'm awful."

Wally put on her most non-judgmental face. It must have worked, or Kelley must have been ready to unburden herself, because she explained. "I called his office to find out why I didn't get my check this month and his secretary told me about his death."

Kelley fidgeted with the fringe on a multihued knit afghan. "Look, I know you are Rachel Morris's mother and I feel like I can trust you. I didn't really write those letters. Keith did. Do you think I could get in trouble for sending them?"

"Why?"

"Why did I send them for Keith or why did he want them sent?"

"Answer whichever," Wally said, hoping for a breakthrough and anxious to get on with it. "I'm not particular."

"Well, I sent them because Keith asked me to and paid me five hundred dollars to mail each of them. It was supposed to continue right through the summer, every few weeks. I'm not sure why he wanted them sent, but I got the impression it had to do with that woman who has a fencing company."

"What makes you think that?"

"I saw them together in a diner in Union. She was wearing a shirt from her company, Alberta Dellaquan Fencing. Isn't that a funny name? Otherwise I'd never have made the connection. I'm thinking he wanted those letters sent so people who live up by the quarry would want to call her and get new fences."

Wally was impressed by her reasoning. It might well be the truth. She wondered, though, why Keith had made such a big commitment to helping Alberta. Was the rumor about them getting back together true? Or was there some other reason?

"Your house is decorated so beautifully," Wally said as she stood up to leave. "It's just perfect."

"Thanks, but not exactly. My bathroom needs to be gutted, although I can't do it now that Keith isn't paying me any more. That's the last thing I needed to do here, then I could have sold it and started decorating another one."

While Wally was horrified by the thought of moving and decorating all over again, she knew several people who liked to do that. Some people didn't do it for the money. They just needed change. That was probably why her friend Louise had lived in five different houses in town since Wally knew her. Not only did Louise learn about houses hitting the market as soon as they were listed, since she was a real estate agent, but she loved to decorate. She felt her surroundings defined her and she was not a stagnant person. Wally chose not to think Louise was implying that people who didn't crave change were sticks in the mud.

"Give my regards to Rachel," Kelley said, as she walked her to the door. Almost as an afterthought she added, "I hope some of what I told you helps."

Wally nodded appreciatively. She wasn't sure whether it would or not, but at least it explained a few things. Too bad it raised just as many questions as it answered.

After calling the fencing company, Wally found Alberta Dellaquan at work on a job site on the opposite side of the quarry from Gabe's house. There was no cliff at that point and although the house was quite far up on the hill, it was on level ground with that part of the quarry.

Wally introduced herself to Alberta, who immediately got her guard up. Knowing that she would get few useful answers from the woman if she stayed so tense, Wally made some idle chitchat, starting with wondering why the homeowners were putting up the fence.

Alberta pulled off her work gloves. "The plans for

the quarry construction called for the area behind this new fence to be sheared off and a retaining wall built. The homeowners wanted their yard fenced before a dangerous situation happened."

"I guess they don't really need that now," Wally said.

"You don't know that," the young woman said, somewhat defensively. "Is there something I can do for you?"

"I was wondering about your relationship with Keith Hollis."

"Look, I told the police. I was not sleeping with him. We were just friends."

"That's what I heard. But I also understand that he was helping you with your business."

"Who told you that?"

No one had, not specifically, but Wally felt she had hit her mark. And it made sense—Keith was paying Kelley Perren to send those letters which directly benefited Alberta's business, as well as Keith's conviction that the town was better off with him owning that quarry than having it be potentially dangerous municipal land. The one thing she hadn't figured out was why Keith was willing to spend so much money on the letters, since he was cash strapped to begin with. That was the question she posed to Alberta.

Alberta scowled. "Oh, believe me, he wasn't only doing it out of the goodness of his heart. I had to kick back a percentage of every job we did in Grosvenor to Keith."

"But not five hundred dollars."

For a moment the only sound was of Alberta's crew working on the fencing. "So you know about Kelley?"

Wally nodded.

"Look, I know I was a stupid kid when I got involved with Keith. But now I am a self-made woman and I was doing business with the big boys. Maybe I was wrong to go along with Keith, but he had co-signed my loan, and I couldn't turn him down. And those letters really did help me get business."

Scare tactics and strong arming business practices were probably what got Keith killed, but Wally didn't say that out loud. Instead she asked Alberta who might have wanted Keith dead.

"I don't know. Maybe lots of people. My brothers were pretty mad at him, but I don't think that after all this time they'd try to go after Keith. And I didn't do it—fifteen people on Fire Island can vouch for that."

So Wally had heard. "That sounds like fun, going out there with all those friends."

Her face was grim. "I wouldn't exactly call them friends, more like acquaintances. But they can vouch for me." This woman who had once been so young and stupid that she got involved with a married man, and bragged about it on the back of a check she was sure the man's wife would see, was older now, and had made a life for herself, but she seemed lonely. Wally wondered if she had found any happiness at all.

Chapter Seventeen

Dominique seemed tense when Wally met her for coffee before day camp, but she made the necessary small talk while they waited for the waitress to bring their orders. Although Dominique ordered a large chocolate chip muffin to go along with the coffee, Wally, whose clothes felt a little snugger lately, resisted temptation.

"It isn't as good as what you bake," Dominique admitted. "You aren't missing much." She kept eating, however, so Wally assumed the burden of conversation.

"In answer to your question," she said, "Rachel is leaving next Tuesday. Adam will be home from his business trip and they'll have one more week until the baby comes."

Dominique took a sip of her coffee. "You're probably wondering why I called you this morning."

Wally had been wondering, and worrying. She expected bad news—that Gabe Ferry was about to be arrested. It had been so frustrating that she couldn't find anything to help clear him the way she had found a way to clear Merle's daughter. Dominique's call confirming the story Lara had told about the cat and its owner had been most welcome. But so far there had been no corroboration of Gabe's alibi, and his dog wasn't talking. Detective Davis had it all worked out, in his mind, Dominique told Wally. He came up with a scenario that Gabe had gone home to let his dog out, found Keith on his property and flown into a rage, picked up the shovel and swung it at Keith's head. Pushing him off the cliff had come later as well as wiping off the shovel.

"There just isn't any other viable suspect," Dominique said. "If it helps, our case is weak. Just circumstantial. We may not get an indictment."

Wally had not told Dominique about her conversation with Bucky. If she did, she might head off Gabe's arrest while they checked Bucky out. But it seemed wrong to mention, since she didn't believe he had murdered Keith, like sacrificing one person for another. On the other hand, she was withholding information. If Bucky had something to do with the murder, she was allowing Gabe to be under suspicion for nothing.

Dominique narrowed her brown eyes. "What? No argument? No protest?"

"You have to do what you have to do."

"Are you saying you believe Gabe did it?"

"Absolutely not."

"There just isn't enough evidence that we can trace," Dominique said, apparently in defense of the police. "The site was messed up by the construction. There were only smudged prints on the shovel, and the one tiny fiber we found is, so far, untraceable. It could have come from any of thousands of jackets."

It was a surprise to Wally that they had anything like that. She knew Dominique was going out on a limb to even mention it. "What color?" she asked, hoping that she'd spot it somewhere and miraculously identify the murderer. Too bad it was July and most people didn't wear jackets. Then again, someone had it in his possession the night of the murder. Maybe Bucky? Maybe he was lying?

"The color is called fawn. It was a Dagmar Hawk golf jacket."

"What is that?"

"He's a new designer, and he's very hot."

Wally shook her head sadly. "I am so out of touch."

"Don't let it bother you. Most people haven't heard of him yet. But his jackets have been selling like crazy."

"And you think Gabe Ferry bought one?"

Dominique shrugged. "They sell in all the high-end stores, and if you ask me, they look like any other men's jacket. But the color is attractive."

"You could tell all that about the jacket from one thread?"

"I couldn't, but the people in the lab are certain. They showed me a picture once they had identified it."

"Does Gabe own a jacket like that?"

"Not that we've found. But he could have gotten rid of it by the time we searched his house."

"Anything else?"

"Maybe. I don't know. Listen, I don't know how familiar you are with the quarry but there is something that puzzles our investigators."

"What is it?"

Dominique pulled out a sheaf of photos from a folder that was next to her on the restaurant bench. "Take a look at this."

Wally looked at three pictures. Two were of normal everyday trees and shrubs.

There was a huge rock outcropping in the third picture that Wally thought she recognized from her nature walks in the quarry. The photograph also showed a shrub which looked as if someone had fallen on it, with broken and twisted branches. She sucked in her breath. "Is that where Keith landed?"

"No. That would be impossible. But those are fresh breaks. We just don't know what it means. I know this is farfetched but I'm grasping for any possibilities. Do you have any ideas?"

Wally shook her head. "I wish I did."

Wally stopped by Gretchen Ralston's on the way home from the nursery day camp. Gretchen seemed pleased to see her and invited her in for some iced tea.

"I don't know what you did, but Bucky told me everything. I'm so relieved."

"I'm happy to hear that." Wally struggled to find a

way to phrase her next question. She thought about saying she was looking at jackets for Nate and wondering how Bucky liked his fawn-colored Dagmar Hawk jacket but she couldn't make herself form those ridiculous words.

"Is something wrong?" Gretchen asked. The smile she'd worn had disappeared.

"I don't think so," Wally said. "There's just one thing. I need an honest answer."

Hesitant, Gretchen nodded.

"Does Bucky have a fawn Dagmar Hawk jacket?"

Gretchen looked puzzled, but she shook her head. "He has a lot of jackets. And several golf jackets. But no Dagmar Hawk. They are just a bit too trendy for my husband."

Wally was surprised that Gretchen knew about the new jackets and felt even more behind the times.

"And," Gretchen continued, "he tends to wear more navy than beige or brown." She stood up. "We can go look in the closet if you like."

Wally wanted to be thorough, so that she could be positive, even though she believed Gretchen. They both took a quick look in the hall closet. Wally saw several jackets, mostly navy. One had the country club logo on it, and Wally noticed that Bucky had a matching baseball cap. There were no fawn-colored jackets.

"That clears him for good, doesn't it?" Gretchen asked, walking Wally to the door.

"I guess so. Please don't mention the jacket to anyone, though."

* * *

Wally was about halfway home when she saw Leigh Fried standing in front of her house which bordered the low end of the quarry. She was talking over the fence to her neighbor Cyd Buxton. Leigh waved for Wally to pull into her driveway.

"How was Africa?" Wally asked, getting out to give Leigh a hug and Cyd a wave.

"Unbelievably fabulous. The best trip of our lives."

"Did you take a lot of pictures?"

"You can't imagine. Marty is inside right now transferring the pictures to the computer. Will you and Nate be able to come over soon to look at them?"

"We'd love to, but Rachel is staying with us until Tuesday. She's having her baby any day. Can I call you?"

Leigh nodded and Wally got back into the car. She always enjoyed seeing the Frieds' pictures but she didn't think she could sit still for them with so much on her mind. It would have to wait.

"We'll be here," Leigh promised.

"I have lunch all ready, Mom," Rachel said, when Wally came into the house. "Dad is on his way from the barn."

A glance at the table told Wally there was more up than just lunch. Rachel had gone to a lot of trouble, making the table pretty with some flowers from the yard, and using fancy placemats and napkins. "This looks lovely. What's going on?"

"I don't know exactly. I just felt the need to make things cozy. In fact, I feel the need to do that at my own house."

Wally recognized the nesting instinct. With Rachel getting close to her due date it made sense that she was getting ready. She wondered if the baby was going to make an early appearance. "But Adam isn't home yet. Are you sure you want to be there alone?"

"I called him last night. He got on an eight A.M. flight."

"Okay then. Dad and I will pack you up and bring you home after lunch. We'll get you all set up. Then we'll wait until Adam gets there."

"Maybe that's a good idea."

Nate, who had come in on the end of the conversation, raised an eyebrow. He seemed just as surprised as Wally that Rachel was agreeing to let them drive.

Nate took Rachel and Jody home in their car while Wally drove her own car to a store to restock Rachel's fridge. Adam arrived at three just after Wally made sure that Rachel's family had everything they needed for the duration of the pregnancy and some time beyond. Then she and Nate headed home.

Wally called Louise when she arrived. "I think it will be soon."

"Then you'd better make some progress solving the murder case."

Of all the things Wally had expected her friend to say, that was not one of them. "You can't be serious. How do you expect me to do that?"

"I don't know. You always find a way."

"I think I'll leave it to Dominique. She's quite capable."

"Tell that to Petra and the kids."

An unpleasant feeling passed over Wally. "I'm sure she knows I'm doing what I can."

"Suit yourself," said Louise, in the annoying tone she sometimes got when she wasn't getting her way. "But there will be an awful lot of disappointed students if their hunky professor doesn't come back to school because he is rotting in jail for something he didn't do. Unless you think he did murder Keith. Then I guess you can just let it go. Case solved. He's guilty."

"He isn't." Wally said. "But Dominique doesn't have anything to work with to prove someone else did it. That would be Gabe's best defense."

"Um hum."

"So if I could find . . . wait, what are you doing to me? My daughter is about to have a baby and you want me to run all over town asking people questions to try to find out who killed Keith?"

"As long as you have a plan," Louise said. Wally could hear her smiling, and smugly at that.

"I'll see what I can do," Wally told her. "But I'm making no promises. There are priorities."

"Whatever."

"Interested in helping?" Wally challenged. "You know many of the main characters."

"Just tell me where and when."

Wally admired Louise's enthusiasm. But they had to have a plan.

"Okay, let me call you back. I have to do a little thinking."

"Don't think too long. Your daughter is about to have a baby."

"You are exasperating, Louise Fisch," Wally said. "I'll call you."

It was time for a list. Wally had talked to many of the people involved in the case, but not all. Ronny Walsh, who owned the house where Keith was staying at the time of his death, topped the list, since he knew so many of the players. Wally hoped he would have more to say about Keith and his comings and goings. If possible, Wally hoped to talk to Coach Morgan and Dr. Fakhouri. She also wanted to talk to the poker players, if possible, but talking to Ronny might give her a better idea whether that would be necessary.

Another candidate was J.J. Ogden who knew Keith the longest, other than his sister. He might have some insight that everyone else had overlooked, especially since he had actually seen Keith that evening. She also wanted to follow up with Keith's secretary, as well as his old secretary.

Nate came into the kitchen and helped himself to a kiss on Wally's neck. While he was there he did a little reading over her shoulder and sat down next to her at the kitchen table.

"I see you have some ideas about the case," he said. "I'm sure Gabe will appreciate that."

"I hope so, although I don't really have anything to go on. I just thought someone should talk to these other people."

"You?"

"Louise is going to split it with me."

One look at Nate's face told Wally that her husband thought that might be a mistake. "She's good at getting people talking," Wally said.

"That's true, I suppose. But I don't think she is nearly as clear-sighted as you."

Wally stood and gave her husband a kiss on the cheek. "That's sweet. I'll keep it in mind."

When she called Louise to make the arrangements, though, she learned she'd be on her own. Louise had picked up a new big-budget client, being moved by a corporation anxious to have its new employee settled as quickly as possible. She wouldn't have time to interview anyone.

"Hmph," Wally said, sitting down next to Nate. He put down the book he was reading and raised an eyebrow.

"She can't do it."

"Who?"

"Louise. She's too busy with a new client. That's great for her, but it means I have to talk to all these people by myself."

"You could let the police handle it," Nate suggested.

Wally frowned at him. Nate reached over and smoothed her brow, then gathered her into his arms. "I might be convinced to give you a hand, that is, if you make it worth my while."

Wally jumped up. "Would you? That would be wonderful! You'd be so good at it, oh this is great, I can't wait to tell Domin—" She was unable to talk anymore because Nate had his finger on her lips. She moved his hand and gave him a big kiss. "You are the best," she said, when she was finally able to talk again. "Let's make a plan."

The way it worked out, Nate was going to talk to Keith's secretary and see if he could get a lead on the former secretary, the one who had left only six months before Keith died, and had been there since he started his own business. He would also talk to all the business partners who had been investing in the quarry development. Wally would talk to everyone else on her list. It was too late to make any calls to set up appointments, though, so Wally and Nate found other things to do for the rest of the evening.

Wally drove over to Ron Walsh's offices. His architectural firm was in an old bank building and his office was in the bank vault. As Wally stepped over the threshold, she became the focus of all the young people in their cubicles lining the balconies that ran along the walls midway to the vaulted ceiling.

"Come on in," said Ron. "Don't mind them. They've heard about your reputation."

"I beg your pardon?"

"Sorry. It's my fault. I told them I was going to be questioned by our local detective. These kids thrive on gossip. I think it helps their creativity."

"I'm impressed with the way you set up the office," Wally said from the doorway. She looked up at them. "They look as if they are floating up there, and you can still see the whole ceiling."

"That's what I was trying to do. I needed more space than we had on the ground level, but I didn't want to chop up the building. Would you like to go on the balcony to see what it looks like? There is a great view of the mosaic design on the floor."

A wave of nausea rose from Wally's midsection and moved north. "No thanks. I have issues with heights."

"Oh, okay." He waved her to a seat. "Now tell me how I can help you."

"I am trying, in my own small way, to find out who killed Keith Hollis, although"—she paused, realizing how ridiculous that sounded and how presumptuous, as if she had a clue—"I'd settle for just clearing Gabe Ferry."

"I don't think I can help you with that. I don't know anything about his involvement."

"That's okay, I didn't think you would, although it would have been nice. What I'm trying to do is find out about the other men living in your house and whether you or one of them know anything helpful."

"The police have talked to them and to me. I don't know what there is to add. Keep in mind, I barely ever stay there. I am staying at my fiancée's because it is closer to the house we're building."

"You're moving out of town?"

Ron nodded. "She works in Somerset and we're splitting the difference. There is much more land out there, too. I'm building the house of my dreams. Do you want to see a picture?"

Without waiting, Ron pointed to a rendering of a

beautiful house, with huge windows, decks, gardens and pathways. Wally practically drooled.

"Keith was living in a dream house, wasn't he?" she said. "Did you design it?"

"Yes. That's how we met. And why it was so hard for me that he and Tori were splitting. I thought they'd live there forever."

"You let him live in your house?"

"I did. Maybe I shouldn't have. Maybe they would have worked it out. But he convinced me." Ron frowned.

"What did he do?"

"Nothing really. He pointed out that I had two other guys doing the same thing."

"He couldn't afford his own apartment?"

"Sure he could, but he was being careful with money, he told me, because of the quarry building."

"Did he offer to let you design some of the homes?"

Ron paled. "He did. I would have let him live there anyway, but when Keith wants, er, wanted something he used all his ammunition, even if he could have kept some of it in his arsenal."

That reminded Wally of something Keith's sister, Peggy, had said. Keith could go for the jugular, or at least the Achilles' heel, of a person, if he felt it necessary.

"Did he have something on the other men in the house?"

"I don't know. But I'm reasonably sure it wasn't one of them. From what I heard the police say they all have alibis."

"Do you know the poker players?"

"Keith introduced us. Strange mix of people."

Wally knew that was true. The group was comprised of Neal Dawson, Graham Fraser, who was seeing Merle, Keith's ex-wife, and someone named Boomer Revere, although Wally was willing to bet that wasn't the name on his birth certificate. She knew from Dominique that Revere was in the clear, and that Neal Dawson also had a credible alibi.

"Why do you say that?"

"Don't misunderstand me, I don't have anything against the guys. They all seem okay. But Dawson and Fraser, the ones he said he knew in high school, are kind of everyday guys, not flashy like Keith at all, although they were all supposedly in what we'd now call a garage band together. And Boomer reminds me of the people in the movie *Animal House.* In fact, Keith and Boomer almost came to blows one night over it."

"What happened?"

"Keith was losing and he started calling Boomer a fat slob and saying a few other unkind things. Using his whole arsenal yet again. Apparently Boomer didn't like that. Keith paid for the damage, though."

"So Boomer was really angry at Keith," Wally mused. "But he couldn't have done it."

"I don't think those other guys could have done it, either."

"Did you spend any time with them?"

Ron shook his head. "No, not really. It's just an impression I get. I see them as two nice guys, still friendly years after high school, who have taken different paths but still want to get together."

Wally resisted the urge to tell him to leave the assessment of the suspects to the professionals and had to stifle a guilty giggle. She wasn't any more of a detective than the man in front of her. At the very least, someone would have to talk to Graham Fraser. Merle herself had said that she didn't meet up with Graham until after the fireworks were over. It was possible he would have had time to kill Keith.

"Did Graham or Neal ever raise their voices the way Boomer did?"

"Not that I ever saw. They don't seem like really passionate people, not the way Boomer was that night. It never seemed to bother them when Keith acted superior or cool. I think they both had his number."

Wally wondered exactly what number that was. "Thanks Ron," she said, when she was leaving.

"Did I help?"

"In a way, I guess. I have a clearer picture of what went on at your house." She smiled at the thought of what Georgia Dewey, the nosy neighbor, had said was going on. For a minute she considered sharing it with Ron, so they could both have a good laugh and lighten the situation with Keith's death and all, but decided against it. It was too weird.

Since there was nothing else Wally could do for the day, she went home and made Nate a nice dinner, featuring only adult food. It wasn't that she didn't love having Jody visit, but her granddaughter's tastes had not yet become any more sophisticated than macaroni and cheese.

During the meal Wally mentioned that the Frieds were back from their trip to Africa. "They seemed anxious to show us the pictures," Wally said. "I told them I'd call them when we have a minute."

Nate blinked. "Um, okay, we can go see them someday."

"Come on, don't be like that. You know they'll be great. And Marty would be so forlorn if we didn't go."

"Fine. What's wrong with right now?"

His one-hundred-and-eighty degree change of attitude unnerved Wally, but just for a moment. "We have too much going on. I couldn't possibly concentrate."

"It might be just the thing for you," Nate said. "I'm going to call them."

Leigh was standing on the walk when they arrived. They followed her into the Tudor style house and into the den where Marty had hooked his computer into a big screen TV.

Marty saw Wally and Nate and winked. "Are you here to be the first to see our pictures?"

Nate shook his hand. "Yes. Everyone else will be so jealous."

Leigh, who was bringing in a tray of cold drinks, rolled her eyes. "You're probably the only ones who are willing to look at them. Everyone else always asks where all the people are. Marty doesn't take pictures of people. He photographs places and things."

The first picture came on the screen. There was a large lake and what looked like thousands of birds. "Oh, I know where this one was taken," he mumbled, half to himself.

Wally was disappointed. "These are black and white."

"They are. I like both black and white and color pictures. When I do my final prints, the pictures may be in black and white, but they were shot in color. It gives me options, and makes it crisper when I keep the tones black and white."

Marty ran through some pictures at a rather fast clip and Wally had to concentrate to see them all. She decided she didn't need an explanation about any of Marty's fancy photography tricks.

Leigh cleared her throat. "Do you think you could possibly turn the color on? I know your masterpieces will be in black and white but most people want to see pictures in color."

"I'll be happy to." He hit a few keys on the computer and instantly the pictures were in gorgeous color. There was the light brown of the dried veldt, the blue of the sky and water and the bright colors of the animals and birds. The pictures were breathtaking.

"Here comes another roll," said Marty. "Let's see where in the trip they're from."

The browns and tans were replaced by brilliant fireworks. "This is the roll from July fourth," Marty said, unnecessarily. "Do you want to see them?"

"Yes!" said all three members of Marty's audience. He ran through the roll quickly, obviously in a hurry to return to Africa.

Suddenly the screen was filled with green. "Wow," said Nate. "Is that a rainforest?"

"Uh, no," said Marty. "That's the quarry. This is still the roll of fireworks. I finished it off the next morning."

Wally turned to him. "You were in the quarry that morning?"

"Yes, I went out the back door and walked about halfway in. Why?"

"Didn't you hear what happened to Keith Hollis?"

The Frieds looked at each other. "Maybe you should tell us."

The couple was horrified by what they heard, especially about Gabe, with whom they were friendly. "Are you going to find the murderer, Wally?" Leigh asked.

Wally felt her face burn. "I don't . . ."

"She's doing everything she can to find out who did it," said Nate. "But tonight I'm trying to distract her."

"Well, then," said Marty, "back to the pictures."

Wally looked closely at the picture. At first all she could see was green. Spring this year had been particularly wet and it had rained right through June. The weather had dried up since then, and July so far had been lovely, if hot. Lawns were beginning to dry out now, but back when the pictures were taken on the morning of July fifth, everything had been verdant.

"I was playing with the sunlight so I took a few pictures in each direction," Marty said. He pointed. "These were facing east, these south, north here, and here are the ones facing west. The sun had been up for a while, so I didn't exactly get the effect I wanted."

The pictures were mostly of trees, with some sky visible between the densely packed leaves. The one facing west was the least light, maybe because of the position of the sun.

Leigh was looking at the screen. "Do you have pictures taken below where Gabe Ferry lives?"

Marty gave his wife a loving, but baffled, look. "If I did, wouldn't I have seen Keith's body?"

"Oh, yeah." Leigh shook off her embarrassment and went to freshen everyone's drink. She also brought back a coffee cake, fresh from the oven, which explained why the house smelled so wonderful.

The last picture showed the rock outcropping Wally was familiar with and some shrubs and trees. But there was something odd about the picture.

"That's it for the quarry," Marty said. "Let's go back to Africa."

Wally soon stopped worrying about the picture because the next ones were so beautiful. "I can't believe you could get so close to those animals," she said. "Weren't you afraid?"

Leigh shook her head. "Telephoto lens. We weren't that close."

There were many pictures and Wally sat back to watch them all as they came up on the screen. But her mind kept going back to that picture in the quarry. It was quite late when they were finished, but Wally asked if Marty could find that last quarry picture again. Once it was on the screen she knew why it had bothered her. "What is that?" she asked, pointing at an oddly placed shadow.

Marty shook his head. "I don't know. Maybe a black plastic bag."

"It shouldn't be there," Wally said.

"I'll say," said Leigh. "But the wind blows a lot of stuff in there." She shook her head.

"It's late," said Nate. "Thanks so much for the show. The pictures of Africa are spectacular, even if my wife likes the one taken out your back door the best."

"I think it's different," Wally said.

"What is?"

"The picture in the quarry. It's different."

"From what?"

"From the one Dominique showed me. It's the same shot, but it isn't. Something is different. They could only have been taken a few hours apart. How could that be?"

Nate looked at Wally, then at Marty. "She might have something. Do you think you could show it to the police?"

"Sure. I'll burn it onto another CD. Where do I take it?"

"Take it to Dominique Scott at the police station. She will know what to do." Wally was excited now. Maybe there would be a usable clue here. "Thank you," Wally said. She felt better than she had in a while. "For everything."

When they left Wally was hoping there would be something in the picture to give the police a clue to the murderer. Otherwise, she was worried that Gabe Ferry was going to be missing the start of the next semester in school, and maybe the rest of his life.

Nate stopped by a black and white photograph on the wall. "One of yours?" he asked Marty.

Marty nodded.

"Out the back door?"

"Yes."

"Unbelievable."

Once Nate had moved closer to the door, Wally was able to see what he meant. It was a picture of a buck with a full rack on his head looking majestically at something in the distance. It made her hope all the more that there would be no more talk of building in the quarry.

Chapter Eighteen

Nate had a pleased-with-himself look on his face when Wally got home. "Mission accomplished," he said.

"You talked to Keith's old secretary already?"

"And his most recent one, and Dr. Ogden."

"You're kidding."

"No."

"What did you find out?"

"Come and sit next to me and I'll tell you." He sat on the couch and opened his arms for her.

Snuggling in next to him, even though she was nearly jumping out of her skin in anticipation of what he had to say, she waited for him to begin. He did, but it wasn't what she had been waiting for.

"Stop nuzzling my neck," she said, "and tell me what they said. Go in order and don't leave anything out."

"Fine," Nate said, assuming a business tone. "First I

saw Tara Wafer, Keith's old secretary, who, by the way, is not old. Maybe thirty-five. She told me that she quit because she knew that Keith wasn't keeping the investors' money in an escrow account and that she didn't want to wait for him to be convicted of something, or put out of business, to start looking for a new job. She found a good one and quit, as simple as that."

"Wow. You do good work."

Nate dipped his head. "Thank you, ma'am."

"Anything else?"

"You are the demanding one, aren't you? And yes. I asked if there was insurance on the quarry venture and she said yes. She didn't know the terms, though."

"I am so impressed. I'd never have thought of that."

"Insurance is one of my businesses, might I remind you?"

"So noted. Go on."

"Next I went to see Gigi, Keith's newlywed and newly unemployed secretary. She is a lovely girl, very astute. She said she was convinced that the deal with the partners was fine. She had just issued a statement to everyone."

"That's interesting. Did she show you a copy?"

"Yes. It looked fine to me. And she showed me a copy of the keyman life insurance policy."

"It didn't say anything like he'd be worth more dead than alive, did it?"

"Well, of course not. But if Keith died, the investors would be paid the value of their investments."

Wally mulled that over for a bit. "Keith's sister Peggy said some investors were pulling out."

Nate shook his head. "There was just one as far as I know."

"Who?"

"Dr. Ogden."

"He asked for his money back?"

"He never paid."

"Oh, that's odd," said Wally. "Why not?"

"What do you mean?"

"Why did Dr. Ogden decide not to invest?"

"How should I know?"

"You went to see him."

Nate nodded. "I did. But just to verify what Gigi told me. He no longer had any connection to the venture. He told me he had told the police that, too, and that on the night he was killed Keith was still trying to interest him in putting in the money. They were up at the school yard overlooking the quarry together before Dr. Ogden left to go meet his children at the fireworks."

Wally didn't say anything for a minute. She had heard from Dominique about the meeting on the evening of the murder. Several questions had popped into her head about that. Nate had missed an opportunity to ask those questions. But he had tried his best and she couldn't fault him for not thinking the same way as she.

"Great job," she told him, snuggling closer. "My detective."

She tossed and turned all night, going over and over the questions she would have liked to ask Dr. Ogden. Since he was the last person to admit to seeing Keith alive, there must have been something else he could have helped resolve. Finally, at about three, Wally got out of bed and went downstairs to write down all the questions. Once she did that, she was able to get some sleep.

At twenty minutes after eight Wally woke up. Nate's side of the bed was long empty, since he had an early meeting, and had obviously forgotten to reset the alarm. Wally had to be in school at ten minutes to nine, so with a cry of dismay that only Sammy heard, she jumped into the shower. She was still trying to explain her strange behavior to the bewildered dog, and her very wet head which would have to air dry, instead of being blown and coaxed into at least partial submission, when she closed the back door and got into her car. She had noticed that the answering machine was blinking as she grabbed her car keys, and figured that someone had called while she was in the shower, but she had no time to listen to the message. Only one message was important enough to be late to school for, and to make sure that wasn't the message she didn't get to hear, Wally pulled out her cell phone in the school parking lot and dialed Rachel's number. Adam answered and said, no, they hadn't called. Whatever it was could wait.

After a busy and noisy morning with the children, Wally went home. Again she apologized to Sammy, as she let him out, for her erratic behavior earlier. He didn't seem to care, and she pushed the answering machine button.

"Wally," said the voice, which belonged to Dominique, "we have compared the pictures taken by your friend Mr. Fried with those taken by the forensic investigators and there is a difference. The dark object in Mr. Fried's picture does not appear in ours. Also, the shrubbery is undamaged in Mr. Fried's pictures. He swears the time of the picture is correct. Since we can't figure out why there would be a difference, we are attempting to blow up the picture. So far, all we can tell is that it seems to be a baseball cap, dark blue or black. Call me."

Wally had flashes of navy baseball caps. She'd seen several, recently. Aside from Yankees caps, which many people in town wore, Wally had seen one on Gabe Ferry, and one in Bucky Ralston's closet. Whose cap could it have been in the quarry? If the cap had something to do with the murder, then had she been wrong to eliminate those two men? How might the cap be involved?

Dominique wasn't in when Wally called. Frustrated, she began going over the questions she had come up with during the night. The phone rang and Wally ran to get it. But instead of being the police detective, it was Rachel. "I heard you called."

"I was worrying that you had called." She explained about oversleeping and having to leave the house without getting the message on the answering machine. Rachel laughed. "At least I wasn't late," Wally said. "But my hair is awful." She began to consider putting one of Mark's old baseball caps on her head to hide it. Since she was on the portable phone, she headed upstairs.

"What are you doing now?" Rachel asked.

"Why, did you want me to do something for you?"

"No. Not for me. I wanted you to get some rest. Pretty soon you'll be pressed into Grandma duty again and you sound a little frazzled."

"I'm fine. Actually, I'm on my way to Mark's room to look at his hats."

"Hats?"

"Yes. I need one to hide my hair. But here's something interesting. Dominique said something about a baseball cap in the quarry. I'm trying to figure out what it might mean."

"Why don't you leave that to her?"

"Oh, I will. But first I want to ask some questions of someone that someone else didn't think to ask."

"Are you talking about Dad?"

"How did you know?"

"He told me he was acting as a detective yesterday. So he didn't do a good job?"

"He did a great job, mostly. Don't tell him I said he didn't finish it."

"I won't. Have fun. And be careful."

"I will," Wally promised. "And you be careful, too. Stay close to home."

While wondering about the baseball cap, Wally drove over to the office of Dr. J.J. Ogden which was in an office complex not far from the hospital. She was still convinced that as a friend of the victim, and as someone who saw him shortly before his death, he might have a few pieces of information. Nate hadn't asked him any questions at all about relationships Keith might have had, and possible people who might be angry enough at Keith to want to end his life. She realized it was asking a lot to take more of the doctor's time, but she would make it quick.

As she got out of her car she saw a familiar face approaching the office building. For a moment she was stumped about where she knew the man from but it suddenly came to her. He was the man sitting next to Peggy Trinity at her brother's funeral. Wally wondered if he might be able to help her.

"Excuse me," she said, hurrying to catch up with him. He turned and stopped just outside the double doors.

"Thanks," said Wally. "I'm hoping you can help me." She took a moment to catch her breath. "My name is Wally Morris. Didn't I see you at Keith Hollis's funeral?"

The man stared at her. She was a little embarrassed that she had decided to stick a red Grosvenor High School Baseball team cap on her head to cover her Sable Mist-colored mess, and his silence was making her more than a bit uncomfortable.

"I spoke to your husband yesterday," the man said. "Didn't he tell you?"

"You did?"

"I'm Dr. Ogden. He said he was talking to me on your behalf."

Feeling stupid beyond belief as the pieces of the puzzle fell into place, Wally realized that the doctor was the same man who had been sitting next to Keith's sister, Peggy, and niece, Fiona, at the funeral. She congratulated herself on her decision to visit him. Obviously this man would know more about Keith than any of them had realized, since he was an old family friend. He might have had good reason for not paying the money, maybe inside information on something Keith was doing wrong.

Wally stammered an apology. "I have no standing to ask you questions," she added.

"Your husband said the same thing. But don't worry, I know you are trying to help your friend."

"You know about Gabe Ferry?"

"I've met him. I don't think he is the type to commit murder. I don't think too many people are, unless maybe they are forced into a corner."

"Even then . . ."

"Of course, you are absolutely right. Even then, I can't imagine it." His face looked thoughtful, as if he were still trying.

"What I'm trying to do," Wally said, "is find out who might have been pushed, oh sorry, bad choice of words, forced, as you said, into killing Keith."

"I wish I could help with that," Dr. Ogden said. "I've been wracking my brain ever since it happened."

"It must have so been hard on you, since you've known him longer than most of us."

Ogden hung his head. "I've known him almost all my life."

"How did you meet?"

"In high school."

That surprised Wally. Ogden looked older and the lines in his face were deeper than how Wally remembered Keith. Maybe his line of work was harder. "Were you friends with him ever since?"

"Not really. After he donated his kidney to his sister and had to give up football he got a new group of friends. We lost contact."

From what Wally remembered being told, the people who Keith was friends with before his operation were the wild ones, the football players who were so often in trouble. She decided to test her theory. "Oh, did you play football?"

"Yes. All through college."

"While you were taking pre-med courses?"

Dr. Ogden smiled. "I didn't say it was easy."

Smiling, his face took on a softer look. Something about it sparked Wally's memory but she couldn't think of what it was. "When did you and Keith get back together again?"

"A new foursome formed at the club. Keith was one of the four."

"That must have been a nice surprise. You could renew your friendship."

"We didn't have that much in common. He was newly remarried and I was recently divorced. There wasn't much opportunity to socialize off the course."

"But you discussed business?"

"Oh, yes. Keith had a million ideas for investing our money."

"I heard you didn't end up investing. Did you find a problem with his plans?"

"Uh, no, not really. I was happy for him. But my

partner was leaving the practice to move to Florida and I had to buy him out. I only had so much cash."

Wally was amazed at how candid the doctor was being. "That's a shame. So you couldn't be part of the deal?"

Dr. Ogden shook his head. "I had to pass."

"You and Keith were together the night he was killed, looking into the quarry, I understand."

"Yes, but from the school yard area. Not your friend Gabe's house. He wanted to show me what I was missing."

That was kind of mean, Wally thought, if Dr. Ogden couldn't help it. It was probably that kind of behavior that annoyed people.

"Did he mention seeing anyone else that night? What did he say he was going to do after the fireworks?"

A cloud passed over Dr. Ogden's face. "He didn't. I don't know. I wish I had stayed up there with him or brought him back down to the park."

"You shouldn't blame yourself," Wally said. "You couldn't have known." She looked at her watch. "I shouldn't take up any more of your time. Thanks for seeing me."

Someone was coming out the door of the building. A strong breeze released as the door was opened lifting Wally's cap and she had to grab it to keep it from flying off her head. "Um," said Dr. Ogden, seeming distracted by the incident, "you're uh, welcome."

He started to go through the double doors just as Wally's phone rang. She turned away from the door and answered.

"It's me," said Dominique. "It's definitely a baseball cap although they haven't blown it up enough yet to see what's on the front. No one here has any idea what it was doing there."

Wally thought about the cap on her head almost flying off in the breeze from the doorway and remembered the odd breezes that seemed to come up from the quarry at the back of Gabe's property. Maybe it was nothing, but it was mighty strange that the hat was there one minute and gone later. Anyone who would have gone to get the hat would have seen Keith's body lying at the bottom of the quarry, yet the body wasn't reported until the students from the school found it. That had to mean that the killer moved the hat, sometime between when Marty Fried took the picture and the time the pictures were taken at the crime scene. Anyone else would have called the police. Her head spun. That had to be it. It had to belong to the murderer. But how could it have gotten there?

"I have a possible theory," Wally said, taking off her cap and staring at it. "I could go test it out."

"Don't do anything crazy."

"I won't. I'll call you soon. Meanwhile try to find out what's on the front." She closed her phone, turned to go back to her car and collided with Dr. Ogden.

"Sorry," she said.

"No harm done," Dr. Ogden told her. "Your phone call seemed important."

Wally nodded and laughed. "It's not like a patient emergency, but it could be significant. We might be getting closer to finding out who killed Keith. I'm going to go try to see if I can help."

"Good luck," Dr. Ogden said.

Wally drove home, parking across the street from her house and going in the front door, all in order to get in and out quickly, and grabbed an armful of caps from Mark's room, Debbie's room, and the front closet where Nate's were kept. The phone rang while she was on the steps to Rachel's old third-floor room. Caught in between, she opted to let gravity help her and ran down to the second floor to answer the phone.

"Hi, Mom," said Rachel. "I just wanted to let you know that I'm going next door to see Bryndda and her new baby. I didn't want you to worry."

"Thanks. By the way, do you have any baseball caps in your old room?"

"Why?"

"I need them for an experiment. Don't worry, you'll get them back."

"Sorry, Mom. I took them with me when I moved out."

"Don't worry about it. Have fun at Bryndda's. It'll be good for Jody to see the new baby. It'll help with her expectations."

"I'm counting on it."

"Are you taking your cell phone with you? In case we need to reach you?" Wally could have bitten her lip for being so needy about this pregnancy.

"Yes, Mom."

Her tone told Wally her weakness was obvious.

Shrugging it off, she put all the caps in her car and drove up to the quarry.

She parked in the driveway of Gabe's house. There was still yellow police tape near the edge of the property but it had been removed from the other areas. Wally assumed the remaining tape was there to warn people about the fences being down.

Wally stacked up the caps and got out of the car. For a minute she considered ringing the doorbell and asking for help from either Petra or Gabe, but she didn't see either of their cars. She realized she preferred to do it alone, since it was probably a ridiculous theory anyway.

Dominique had confirmed the location of the cap that Marty Fried had inadvertently photographed—just next to the big rock outcropping. It was suspicious that it wasn't located there when the police photographed Keith's body in situ. Moreover, the broken shrubbery had not been crushed in Marty's picture. Maybe Wally's theory was correct, that the wind blowing up out of the quarry could have blown off the killer's hat and caused it to fly to the spot in the picture. Maybe it could be used to trace him, but first the possibility of a link had to be established.

First she walked over to the school yard to see if the cap could have fallen from anywhere else and somehow still be unrelated to the murder. She leaned over toward the six-foot-high fence, safe and secure that she couldn't fall, but still feeling lightheaded looking down into the quarry. Two hats she tried flew off her head, but both flew back behind her, into the yard. The hat couldn't have blown down there from this spot, even if she had been taller.

Wally walked back to Gabe's and went close to the edge. She didn't want to be there at all, and here she was, sticking her neck out literally, trying to see if she could catch a breeze.

She sat down on a rock and put her hats beside her. The ground was a little muddy and she hadn't thought to bring something to rest the hats on. There was probably an old newspaper in her car, she realized, and she went to get it, to put under the caps. There was no reason to make more work for herself having to clean them when she got home.

As she spread out the paper, she moved a few loose rocks to weigh it down. Her hand touched something stuck under one of the rocks. Wally wasn't ordinarily squeamish, but she immediately pulled her hand away. Then she apprehensively looked to see what was there.

It was an antacid wrapper. Just like the ones she had seen Bucky downing so frequently. And he had a navy baseball cap. A feeling of sorrow crept over her, for Gretchen, for Bucky, for Tori and her daughter, for the twins, for everyone involved. She almost wished she hadn't found it at all.

She looked around for a small rock to weigh down the newspaper and protect what she had found, then got back up. Putting one hat on her head and, holding onto a slender tree to quell her fears, she leaned over. The cap immediately flew off her head and sailed into the quarry, landing almost exactly where the dark cap in the picture had been. She tried it two more times and they both went the same way. Later she'd have to go in from below and pick them up, she knew, but for now she had to tell Dominique about the caps and the antacid wrapper. She took out her phone and realized she must have turned it off after she finished talking to Dominique earlier. She turned it on feeling jittery with excitement and dread, waiting anxiously for the phone to be ready to dial.

The detective answered on the first ring. "Are you alright?" Dominique demanded.

"Dominique, I found something. It's important." Suddenly the tone of Dominique's voice sank in. "Why do you sound so upset?"

"Nate called, and he said that Rachel had called and needed you. She didn't know where you were and you weren't answering and she told Nate something about hats."

"Is she in labor?"

"I don't know. But I do know that we got a blowup of the hat. It has a picture of a heart with an electric current running through it."

It hit Wally like a flash. "Oh," she said, "I know who had that hat. It's—"

Suddenly Wally was no longer holding her phone. In fact, it was flying over the edge of the quarry. Wally stared at it in shock, thinking that was probably just what Keith's phone had looked like as it flew over the edge on the night he died. Instantly she was feeling so lightheaded she had to sit down.

She turned and saw why the phone had flown away, and her fear intensified. Standing before her was Dr. Ogden, the person she now remembered seeing wearing the cap with the defibrillation logo, smiling and driving away from Keith's funeral in his Audi sports car, which Wally now saw was parked right behind hers. Realization flooded over her.

"Oh," she said, wishing she hadn't. She sealed her lips to keep them from doing any more damage.

Too late. J.J. Ogden clearly knew she had figured out that he was standing here the night of the murder, not only at the school yard. He was undoubtedly the person who had killed Keith. And he was intent on her not being able to pass along that information. She wished she had told Dominique where she was.

Fearing for her life, Wally tried to stall for time. "Why don't you tell me what happened?" she said, in her best nursery school teacher tone, the one that is not accusatory and holds promise of a reprieve.

Dr. Ogden's face sagged. "It isn't what I wanted." He swallowed hard. "He wouldn't listen," he said. He slipped an antacid out of his pocket and opened it, all the while standing so close to Wally that she had no choice about moving, since the only way she could have gone was over the cliff. "I told him the same thing I told you," he said, while chewing the tablet. "I didn't have the money. You can't get blood from a stone."

"He didn't accept that?"

"He hadn't so far. That's why I asked him to meet me that night. I wanted to make sure he had no distractions so I could get him to listen to me, and really hear what

I had to say. We met and I took him for a ride up to the school yard."

"Did he listen to you?"

"He just stared at me. He started talking about how we had a history together. And how I, more than anyone, knew what a sacrifice he had made when he gave one of his kidneys to his sister. That ended his football career, you know, and his chances for a scholarship. Then he said that I hadn't had that problem, that I went on to college, playing football, and then on to medical school. Now I had a lucrative career, and I had a lot of nerve standing there begging to keep my money to myself. 'You promised,' he said."

Wally just stood there listening. She sensed that she couldn't hurry this story along and doubted that she would have wanted to. Straining her ears, she longed to hear the sound of a car, any car, driving up.

" 'You don't understand,' I told him," Ogden said. " 'I lost all my money when the bottom dropped out of the stock market. Now I have to scratch together enough money to buy out my partner because he is retiring. I don't have any to give you.'

" 'I'm not asking you to give me money,' he said. 'It's an investment. And it would pay more than the stock market did. You'd end up with money, not with nothing.' "

Wally shook her head, trying to seem sympathetic. "He sounds like he was just unwilling to hear your side."

"That's right. I told him there was nothing to invest. My partnership business came first." He had been looking down at the ground but now he looked up at

Wally. "Do you know what he said then? He told me to borrow it."

"What did you do?"

"I just stared at him. I couldn't believe it. Here he was, standing on the edge of a cliff over the hole in the ground he was trying to develop into a moneymaker. But in order to do it, he needed a million dollars from me. I didn't have it.

"I decided I should just turn around and walk away. When he didn't get his money, he'd realize it wasn't coming. At that point it might be too late for him and he'd be out on a limb. But I tried to tell him, and in sufficient time for him to make other arrangements."

"You did try," Wally agreed. "So then what happened?"

"I turned away and walked back to my car. The wind was picking up and I took out my jacket for the ride back down the hill. In the distance, I could see the fireworks starting and it brought back memories of my childhood. We had always gone to see them together, Keith, Tully, Skippy and me. Tully died years ago and Skippy in Desert Storm. I am a successful but temporarily cash-strapped gastroenterologist, and Keith, who was always the leader, is telling me I had to keep my word and invest in his project."

"Did he say anything then?"

Ogden nodded. "He jumped into the car and asked me to drive him over to Gabe's because Gabe has the best vantage point of anyone on the ridge.

"He just wanted to show me one more angle, so I

could understand. So we came over here and I parked in the driveway. We walked back here to the edge.

"The fireworks were going strong as we looked down into the quarry. 'Look,' Keith said. 'Imagine. It will be so exclusive that we'll get triple what the projected prices were. You'll be paid back in no time.'

"I didn't answer. He wasn't getting it. I had no money to give, no way to borrow beyond what I had to buy out my partner. He would either have to get it from someone else or give up on the idea and I told him just that.

"It was windy here, near the edge. I could feel the breeze lifting my baseball cap. I was so proud of that cap, because it was through my efforts, and those of a few others, that defibrillators were made available at all the sports events in town. If someone were struck in the chest causing his heart to stop, we would be able to restart it. People didn't have to die, especially kids."

Ogden pointed down into the quarry. "Right down there a buck stepped into a pool of moonlight. In a way, I realized, it would be nice if no one ever built here.

"Keith didn't see the beauty of that. Instead he turned to me, this time angrily. It was an expression I had seen so many times before. I knew what was coming. He was going to bring up what we'd done, when we were young and stupid. I knew he would never let me go, never let me forget. And he would use it against me if he felt he had to."

Dr. Ogden turned truly sad eyes to Wally. "You have no idea how hard it's been to live with this. I can't keep it inside any more."

Wally didn't move, didn't even blink.

Ogden did, several times. Wally wasn't sure if he was trying to hold back tears. "It was all Keith, always Keith. He'd say we were going to do something and that's what we did. 'We're going to clean up Circle Park tonight,' Keith would tell the cops about the hoodlums who came from out of town to mug our fine citizens. The cops would stay away and let us do what we had to."

"Which was what?"

"We'd run those trespassers back where they came from. Or at least that was the plan." He gulped. "One of them never made it."

Wally got a sinking feeling in the pit of her stomach. Something he'd said a moment earlier came back to her as did what Merle had said about the boys going after the drug dealers and muggers. It sounded dangerous. "You said something happened. Did someone get hurt? Did Keith do it?"

"No, he wasn't part of it, not that night. He was there, but he couldn't fight, because he was still recovering from the operation. But he did drive the car when we dumped that poor kid back on his own turf. And he was part of the meeting that we held, the four of us, to get our stories straight. We had not been there that night, we had not been cleaning the park. We didn't know anything about it."

"What kid?"

"The one who got hit in the chest." Dr. Ogden looked ill and it was clear he was reliving it. He looked down at his hand, which was balled into a fist and visibly shuddered, opening it quickly. "His heart stopped. There was nothing anyone could do, no way to revive him."

Wally had trouble breathing and she had broken out in a sweat. "What happened to him?"

"He died. But the police never really looked into it. We never did that again. And we didn't mean to do it. It was an accident—the single punch to the boy's chest stopped his heart. It happens all the time, from baseballs, and what not. It could have been started again, if only we had known how. I learned that from my training."

Wally's heart was pumping faster than it ever had. She could barely look at Dr. Ogden. He had killed not once, but twice. There was no way she'd get out of this alive.

"The way Keith was acting about the investment brought all those old memories back and suddenly I knew what was coming."

Tears had spilled out of the doctor's eyes but he hadn't backed away from the threatening stance he had over Wally. "What do you think your medical license would be worth if it turned out you were a murderer?' Keith asked me. I reminded him that he'd said we would never talk about that again."

"What did he say to that?" Wally asked, trembling.

"He said 'You said you would invest in my project.'" Ogden looked over at a boulder beside where Wally sat. "I sat down here. There was a backhoe there, and several tools. Keith was still harping on me, telling me what he would do. 'I wasn't involved,' he said, 'at least not in the beating you gave him. I won't be prosecuted. I told you. You're going to pay, one way or another.' I didn't argue. I'm not a lawyer. I was more afraid for myself. I had to stop him somehow.

"I grabbed his arm to try to stop him from talking. 'I'll try to get it somehow,' I told him. He didn't give me a minute to even think, he just kept haranguing me." Ogden's face showed rage, as if he was back talking to Keith. "I began to wish I was somewhere else. Anywhere. I had to stop his diatribe. I reached for one of the spades left nearby. Before I knew it, I had hit him. Again and again. He went down, unconscious. I dragged him here to the edge and rolled him off the cliff. Into his dream. And the finale of the fireworks sent him off to hell."

He took a breath, finally. "I took off my jacket and cleaned my fingerprints off the shovel. I didn't notice that my hat was gone until I was driving home. I went back the next morning to get it." He looked up at Wally, focusing in on the present again and straightening up. "And now I think you understand that as the only other person in the world who knows the truth, you are going to have to follow Keith. I'm not willing to give up my future."

He moved toward her and grabbed Wally's arm, standing her up and dragging her closer to the edge of the cliff. One of her feet slipped over the rim and she grabbed for the tree. Dizziness washed over her, along with nausea.

Then she heard a voice. "Let her go and step away from there," said Dominique. Wally looked over to see the detective standing there pointing her gun straight at

Dr. Ogden. Ryan stood beside her, also pointing a gun, and there were sirens in the distance. Dr. Ogden's grip relaxed immediately. He moved away, and Wally sank down into the base of the tree. Ryan ran over and pulled her to safety.

Chapter Nineteen

When Wally could open her eyes again she saw not only half the Grosvenor police force but also Nate, pale as a ghost. He ran toward her and crushed her in his arms, rocking back and forth. Considering that he could have been yelling, Wally was glad this was the way he was responding to her near demise.

"How did you find me?" Wally asked Nate, not relinquishing her virtual death grip on him.

"Dominique called me after you got cut off. She was worried and she thought you might be trying to figure out how the hat got into the quarry. She said she was coming up here and I jumped in the car and followed. We didn't know about Dr. Ogden."

"I did find out," Wally said, still breathless. "It was the wind. And I know why he had to go get it." She looked around to find Dr. Ogden, and spotted him sitting in the back of a police car. She shuddered.

"He did something as a young man—and Keith, who always went for people's Achilles' heels, was threatening to reveal it."

Nate got himself and Wally up. His face was grim as Wally explained. After a few sentences, though, Wally began to get the impression that she was losing Nate's interest.

"Is something wrong?" she asked him.

He stared at her. "Besides the obvious? Well, there is something else." He looked at Dominique. "We have to go."

Dominique broke away from the other officers and came over to the Morrises. "I need to finish questioning Wally," she said.

Nate shook his head. "Not now. We have to go."

Wally was about to protest when a thought occurred to her. "Is it Rachel?"

Nate nodded.

"We have to go," Wally said to Dominique. "How about if I explain the rest from the car? I can call you."

Nate, who had not let go of Wally's arm and was propelling her toward the car, stopped. "I don't think I could drive and listen to that. Give her a quick explanation of the rest and then we'll go."

Wally gave a thirty-second recap. "I'll fill in details soon," she promised. "Now I have to go be a grandma again."

"He's so precious," Louise whispered, leaning over Wally's shoulder as she cradled the baby close on the day of his brit. "Who do you think he looks like?"

"Himself. Isn't he beautiful?"

"I think he looks like Rachel. He's going to be dark, not like Jody."

Wally looked over at her granddaughter, the proud big sister with her shining red pigtails. "Maybe you're right," she whispered.

Wally looked around at her friends and family, and at Rachel and Adam's friends and family, all crowded into Rachel's living room for the event. Adam, the new baby's father, had the biggest smile on his face that Wally had ever seen, at least since Jody was born. His mother was also beaming, and his father twirled Jody around before giving her a big hug.

Mark had driven Grandma Tillie up to Rachel's and Dominique Scott had taken the day off to be there. Tori Hollis had come, too, with grateful tears for Wally and happy tears for the baby. Everyone else was smiling, especially Debbie and Elliot who were about to become the official godparents of Charlie, really Charles Benjamin. They still glowed from their long vacation/delayed honeymoon and had just come back to town in time for little Charlie to make his appearance.

The ride up to Westchester to be there for the birth had been somewhat harrowing, considering what had so nearly happened to Wally. It all quickly faded into the background, at least until everyone knew that Rachel and the baby were okay. By then Dr. J. J. Ogden had been formally charged and had confessed everything. His life was in ruins.

Now, a week later, everything was calming down. Wally had stopped by the nursery school that morning and been quite pleased. She could tell as she drove up to the synagogue that a big push was on to finish the nursery school. Aside from a van filled with rolls of carpeting, there were three electricians' trucks, a man setting up a saw to cut tile next to a pallet of floor tiles, and two plumbers' vans. Van had assured her it would all be ready by the opening of the fall term. Everything was back to normal and life was going on, maybe better than before. And after several nerve-wracking days worrying about the museum competition, Louise's husband Norman had announced last night at the town council meeting that Grosvenor had won the bid for the museum.

The mohel made a beautiful ceremony. Little Charlie, blissfully sucking on gauze which had been dipped in wine, was welcomed to the world of Judaism. Everyone said, "Mazel Tov."